"Hunter will lead us," Hannah brightened....

"It's worth a try," Mr. Fuller agreed. "But your dog's got to have a leash. Shine your light here." As Hannah held her lantern over his vehicle, the man pulled a short piece of rope from his fishing gear. Hunter complained noisily while being hitched to the snowmobile's handlebars. "Hop on."

Hannah obeyed. Slowly they crept down the ice, following Hunter's fine nose. Then the wind shifted, and Hunter stopped, his nostrils confused by the smell of the snowmobile's exhaust fumes.

"We're lost," groaned Mr. Fuller. "Poor dog can't smell anything but the snowmobile."

"Will we freeze right here?"...

Other books in the
Hannah's
Island
S E R I E S

About the Author

Eric E. Wiggin was born on a farm in Albion, Maine, in 1939. As a former Maine pastor, Yankee school–teacher, news reporter, and editor of a Maine–published Christian newspaper, Wiggin is intimately familiar with the Pine Tree State and her people. He has strived to model Hannah and Walt after courageous examples of the Maine Christian youth he knows well.

Wiggin's ancestors include Hannah Bradstreet Wiggin, and one of his four granddaughters is Hannah Snyder. But his greatest model for the *Hannah's Island* series is Hannah, mother of the prophet Samuel, known for her faith and courage in adversity.

Wiggin's thirteen novels for youth and adults are set in rural or small-town Maine. The woods, fields, and pasture lanes of the Wiggin family farm sloping toward a vast Waldo County bog furnish a natural tapestry for the setting of many of his books.

Author Wiggin now lives in rural Fruitport, Michigan, with his wife, Dorothy.

A Hound for Hannah

Eric Wiggin

Emerald Books

P.O. Box 635
Lynnwood, WA 98046

Contents

Chapter One

Does God Care for Puppies?

"Did Papa say *drown* Missy's puppies?" Hannah Parmenter spoke to Mama in hushed horror as the kitchen screen door banged shut behind her father. Her emerald-green eyes were wide with anger and fear.

"I guess now that you're almost a teen, Papa thinks you're old enough to know about such things," Mama sighed. "Living here on Beaver Island in Moosehead Lake, Maine, we don't have many neighbors close enough to give them to."

"Why can't we just take them to the mainland?" Hannah cried. "Drowning's murder!"

"Isn't that remark a little strong? They're *only* dogs." Mama's blue eyes turned dark and serious as she lovingly patted Hannah's blonde-turning-brown French-braided hair. "Papa's got a lot to do and think about, running this tourist lodge and getting ready for summer vacationers. Why don't you and Walt see if you can find a creative way of taking care of Missy's puppies so Papa won't have to do the

7

dirty work? It's not something your father really wants to do, you know."

Creative. Hannah wrinkled her pug nose and frowned. Then she smiled. When Mama said "creative," Hannah knew she meant for her to think of something fun and original, not just the same old ideas. Already Hannah was sure she'd think of something, Lord willing. "Well," Hannah began, "there's Hunter. I'm keeping *him*—so that takes care of one."

"You've named him already?"

"Sure. When God created the animals, He had Adam name them right away, didn't He?" Hannah said brightly. "I'll go get him!"

Hannah dashed for the wood-burning kitchen stove that sat in the kitchen of Beaver Lodge right next to Mama's bottled-gas cooking range. Even in the dark behind the stove, Hunter was not hard to spot snuggled among his sisters. He was almost white, with brown and tan spots like his basset mother, not just black, like the others, who resembled their Lab father. The other puppies were long-haired girl dogs. But Hunter was one hundred percent flop-eared hound.

And Hannah loved hounds. She adored them, in fact.

"Isn't he *noble*—just like a prince who rescues fair maidens from evil villains?" Hannah had been reading about King Arthur and his royal family. She held the squealing, squirming bundle of baby doggie up for Mama's inspection, straightening Hunter's legs so that Mama could see that he would grow up to be much taller than his close-to-the-ground mother.

"He is grand," Mama agreed, chuckling at Hannah's use of the word *noble*.

"And see his head—real royalty, just like a king!" Hannah lifted her dog's chin so Mama could see the well-formed, intelligent head that must have come from Hunter's father.

"Labrador retrievers do have kingly heads," Mama admitted.

Hannah thought she had Mama convinced.

"But you can't keep a puppy in the house," Mama warned. She shot a glance into the living room where the heavy, leather-upholstered chairs stood ready for the tourists who would come that summer. "Puppies chew. He would ruin every piece of leather in sight, including your father's slippers and a guest's suitcase or two!"

"How about a doghouse?" Hannah suggested, smiling brightly. "That's creative. Walt can help me build it," she added, seeing her brother coming indoors.

"I am *not* going to build any houses for mutts!" Walter interrupted. Since he'd become a teen, Hannah noticed, Walt had become as independent as a coon in a tree and wouldn't play with her as much as he used to. But that was okay. Hannah was growing up, too, so she simply found things to do without her brother.

"Missy sleeps just fine under the porch," Walter added. "That is, she did until she had those dumb puppies!"

"You should talk, Walter!" Hannah hugged Hunter close and glared at her big brother. The puppy accidentally wet the front of her sweatshirt, but she didn't dare let Walt know about Hunter's mishap. To hide the mess, she pulled Hunter closer, folding her arms about the damp, smelly, furry ball of life. Hannah would endure anything under the sun to keep poor Hunter from being drowned.

Besides, the box of puppies behind the stove was really Walter's fault. The first spring day when Moosehead Lake was free of ice, Walt had taken Missy with him in the motorboat to the village of Laketon, a mile down the lake on the mainland. But the wind had come up, making the lake too choppy for him to return safely.

So Walt had spent the night with Aunt Theresa and Uncle Joe Boudreau. Missy had slipped out of Uncle Joe's garage somehow and met a homeless male black Labrador who roamed the streets like a hobo. Weeks later it became obvious that Missy was pregnant.

"Any boy big enough to take a motorboat to Laketon alone would to be able to be responsible for a dog, Sandy," Papa had grumbled to his wife.

"Harry, dogs have independent wills and legs to take them where they want to go when folks are asleep in their beds," Mama pointed out.

Papa realized this was true, and he quickly forgave Walt. Even though he worried about what they would do with her puppies, Papa was proud of Missy, a registered AKA basset. In fact, before she had grown fat from eating scraps from the Parmenters' table, Missy had followed Papa around their island farm.

"It will cost ten dollars apiece, besides a boat trip to the mainland to have the vet put the puppies to sleep," Mama explained to Hannah as soon as Walter, who had come into the house to use the bathroom, left to help Papa mend the pasture fences. "With the money we've spend on the new wallpaper in the guest rooms and the repairs we have to make to the barn, there simply isn't any cash left for such foolishness," Mama said firmly.

Hannah said nothing. Tears flowed freely now. Nobody seemed to understand. *'Put the puppies to sleep' is only a nice way to say 'murder them,'* she thought angrily.

"I love you, honey." Mama pulled Hannah close and hugged her.

"Do...do you love Hunter, too?" Hannah could feel Hunter the hound squirming between them.

"Yes, I guess I *could* love Hunter—why, he's all wet, and you're soaked!"

Hannah smiled through her tears. "Babies *do* wet their diapers."

"I know," Mama said thoughtfully. "You'd better go upstairs and change. *I'll* dry Hunter off and put him back to nurse on Missy."

Mama smiled and reached for a roll of paper towels as Hannah hurried for the stairs.

"Oh, Hannah," Mama called.

"Yes, Mama?" Hannah stopped halfway up the stairs.

"I think Papa will understand about Hunter after all," she said quietly.

As soon as she had put on a clean shirt, Hannah knelt beside her bed. "Dear Father in Heaven," she prayed. "Thank you for helping Mama understand about Hunter. And please help me figure out what to do with his sisters. In Jesus' name, amen."

Mama's right, Hannah told herself as she walked to the window. We can't keep the other pups. It was a fine, sunny Friday afternoon in apple-blossom time, and Hannah's room was getting a bit stuffy. Hannah raised the window to listen to the spring peepers sing their happy song of new life from the marsh along the lake.

Then Hannah heard the far-off snarl of a chain

saw way beyond Papa's cow pasture on the back side of Beaver Island, and she got an idea. Perhaps God was answering her prayer already. "Cool," she said aloud.

Hannah jumped the four steps down to the staircase landing. Then she slid down the banister, racing downstairs to tell Mama her plan to save Hunter's sisters. Though she was eleven-going-on-twelve, Hannah could still act like a tomboy when she had a neat idea.

Chapter Two

Papa Understands

"Hannah *Joy,* Papa will *never* let you go across the island alone. It's not safe!"

"I'm asking you to go with me, Wal-*ter*. I'm not dumb." If it tickled her so when Papa or Mama called her Hannah Joy, why, when her big brother used her middle name, was it the same as calling her a baby? Hannah didn't know why. She only knew it hurt to be teased. Then she'd try to hurt Walt by making fun of his name.

But since she needed Walt's help in saving Missy's puppies, she quickly decided to be nice to him. "Walt," she said kindly, as he started to walk away, "I really *do* want you to go with me."

"Papa won't let us!" Walter growled.

"Oh, yes, he will. He let you go over there *alone* just last week to deliver that part for their chain saw—remember?"

"That was different," Walt answered cautiously. "It was important."

"*This* is important. I'm sure Papa thinks so."

"How do you know?" Walter's eyebrows raised in question. "Did he say so?"

"C'mon. You'll see!" Hannah laughed confidently.

She picked up the box with the three mongrel, Labrador-looking puppies and trudged toward the barn. The sound of hammering and sawing told her that Papa was building a new stall for Ebony, the black stallion he had just bought to pull his wagon loaded with tourists across Beaver Island. Before going inside, Hannah stopped by the barnyard's wooden bars. She held the cardboard box up for the approval of their cream-colored jersey cow.

"M-o-o-o-o-o-o!" They are nice pups, Molly seemed to agree. She rolled her warm brown eyes downward and batted her long, bovine lashes once or twice. "Mohh!" Molly bellowed suddenly. She butted the box from Hannah's hands with her crumpled horn before the girl could step back. Then, acting properly cowlike, Molly stretched her long neck across the bars to munch a clump of witchgrass and dandelions growing beside a post. Molly simply did not care that Hannah had sat down in a cow pie, or that Walt was scrambling to catch the puppies before they could scurry like rats under the barn.

"What's all this?" It was Papa, scratching his head and chuckling as he knocked the barn dust and chaff from his billed cap by whacking it on the knee of his overalls.

"We're keeping Hunter," Hannah gasped, diving for a black, furry puppy that had scurried under the barnyard gate. "Mama says you won't mind." Hannah tucked the squirming creature under one arm while she climbed back outside the gate of fence rails.

"Whoa!" Papa exclaimed. "No hunters until fall. It's against the law." Papa had certainly misunderstood, Hannah thought.

"See. Told y'!" chirped Walt, who obviously wasn't listening to Papa.

"I'd better see what's going on. Guess I didn't hear the man's boat come in." Papa took three strides toward the house.

"Papa, wait!" Hannah called.

Papa stopped. "Hannah, if some hunter thinks he can stay here and hunt out of season, I've got to stop him before your mother rents him a room!"

"But Papa, Hunter's a dog! He's the mostly white puppy—the hound. An' he's *mine!* Mama says it's okay."

Hannah's words came in torrents, like a spring shower. Papa really didn't understand, and Hannah had to set things right.

"Oh? You've named one already?" Papa chuckled, pretending to just catch on. "Guess when pups get names they become special." His brown eyes twinkled merrily as he thought about this. "That does set things in a different light," he added lovingly.

"I've got the three black ones here." Hannah held the box up for Papa's inspection.

"We *still* have a problem, though."

"Yeah," agreed Walt, importantly. "Got t' get rid o' 'em—like you said this morning, Papa."

"Can't...can't I carry them over across the island to where those men from Canada are cutting logs?" Hannah pleaded, fighting back the hot tears that threatened to spill across her cheeks. She wasn't sure what troubled her more—her fear that Papa would drown the puppies or Walt's taunts. "The men go home today—it's Friday—don't they?"

"That they do!" Papa agreed warmly.

"So they might like to have the pups to take home to their families or neighbors. You said yourself that they look like Labradors, and a Lab is a Canadian dog, right?"

"True enough," Papa answered. "I guess it's worth a try. They might take one," Papa agreed, sounding as though he doubted they'd take them all. "Walt, you'll have to go with Hannah."

"I'll go fire up the motorboat. I can get there quick by goin' around the island with the boat!" Walt said as he raced off.

"Wa-alt!" Papa called, causing Walt to skid to a halt. "Hold up! You and Hannah will need to walk through the woods because the motor needs a new sparkplug. Better get going. It'll be dark before you get back if you don't hurry. It's not too far to walk if you stay on the tractor road."

※ ※ ※ ※ ※ ※ ※

"Ze puppies, they will make fine dogs, *non?*" chuckled Jacques LaFonde as he shut off his chain saw. The man with the black beard had worked up a sweat cutting logs for Hannah's father. He was glad for a break.

"*Oui!*" agreed Pierre Pellitier, the other logger. "My Marie, she has wanted a black Labrador for a long, long time. I tell her a woodchopper like me, I can't afford. Labs—they are—how you say in *anglais?*—expensive."

"They're only half Lab," Hannah admitted. She winced as Walt poked her in the ribs as she spoke. "Other half's hound," she added truthfully.

"Hound, eh? Then mebbe they not get so big. But they should make fine house dogs," chuckled

Mr. LaFonde. "I'll take one. *Merci beaucoup!*"

"Well, I *could* take ze other two," Mr. Pellitier agreed, tugging at his red suspenders. "My Marie, she would be pleased. But it's four hours' drive in our old truck to get to my home in Canada. I'm afraid they'd get hungry."

"We have that canned milk, Pierre," Mr. LaFonde reminded his friend. He hurried into the cabin the men shared during the week. Soon he came out with an open can, into which he'd stuffed a milk-soaked rag.

"Ze pups, they'll think this is their *maman*," he laughed.

Then everyone laughed as the lumberjack sat on a log with the puppies, holding the can like a baby bottle and using the milky rag as a nipple. The pups wrestled with each other for a few drops of milk. They squirmed all over Mr. LaFonde's plaid shirt, and even into his bushy beard, so that they seemed to be a part of him. The lumberjack's big, hard hands held the squirming babies gently as he had them take turns at the milk.

Hannah felt that she had never been so happy in all her life as she watched these burly French Canadien loggers feed their furry black babies. The men were tough and strong, but the puppies, delicate and helpless, were perfectly contented to accept them as if they were loving mothers.

"Our Heavenly Father loves even tiny puppies," Hannah said at last. "You and Mr. Pellitier are like angels to them," she told Mr. LaFonde.

Jacques LaFonde looked startled, but Pierre Pellitier, who now was feeding his two pups with the milk-soaked rag, murmured *"oui"* in agreement. "God cares for even ze homeless puppies," Mr.

Pellitier added. "And my Marie, in Quebec, she will love them," he chuckled. "But they'll have to learn to *parlez en Français*," he said, speaking to the pups in a musical French sentence.

Both men laughed as if this were a great joke. Hannah, who was studying beginning French with Mama's help at home, laughed, too.

Chapter Three

Lost on Juniper Bog

"You nearly blew our chances of giving those puppies away," Walt grumbled as he and Hannah hurried toward home. Long, late-afternoon shadows stretched across the narrow woods road Papa had made for his tractor, and Hannah trotted to keep up with her big brother.

"Is that why you poked me in the ribs? For telling that the puppies aren't purebred Labs?"

"Yeah. Who wants mongrel mutts?"

"They *took* the puppies," Hannah pointed out. She couldn't understand why Walt acted so mean. Sometimes Hannah wondered if even Walt knew why he was cross. "You just can't stand it when I'm right," Hannah snapped. Right away, though, she realized she'd said too much.

Just then it dawned on Hannah that the puppies would never see their mama again, and she grew silent. Though she was sure they were going to a good home in Canada, she cried as she realized that the only mother—*maman*, the French logger

19

had said—they'd ever have again would be a dumb old can of milk. She dried her eyes on her sleeve.

"Crybaby," Walt taunted. "Smartypants, too. I'm not walkin' home with a crier."

Walt jogged off, but Hannah did not shout for him to wait. She could take care of herself in these woods. She would just follow the road for a couple of miles. She knew it would come out in the fields behind her home. Hannah trudged on under the darkening sky. The spring air grew cold as the sun sank lower over Moosehead Lake. Hannah wished she'd brought her sweater.

Hannah came to the top of a low ridge, where she could peer far down the road to where it crossed one end of Juniper Bog. Papa had built a section of corduroy road through the bog. He had laid hundreds of short logs side by side so that he could drive his tractor across without sinking into the bog's mud.

It was dark and gloomy down there, where tall alder bushes shaded the road and cattails grew more than head high. Hannah was not afraid to walk through the bog alone, but she remembered the mosquitoes—how hungry they'd been when she and Walt had carried the puppies through there an hour ago.

Hannah couldn't see Walt. Had he gotten past the bog already? Then she spied him scrambling over rocks and ledges on the side of Bald Hill, far above the forest road. Walt was taking a shortcut above the bog, escaping the bloodthirsty mosquitoes and biting midges that burrowed even into your scalp.

Why not? Hannah thought. Papa had not said they *must* follow the road. She had been on Bald

Hill once last summer, right after her family had moved to Beaver Island from Skowhegan. She and Mama had come over here to pick blueberries. She would be smart, like Walt, and avoid the nasty critters in the damp bog.

Few trees grew on Bald Hill, and Hannah found the climb through the low blueberry bushes easy. Soon she was at the top, above the tree-covered island. Far, far to the west the sun hung low over Mt. Kineo, way down Moosehead Lake. Hannah could see the village of Laketon from where she stood. The white spray of a motorboat cutting through the waves toward the village caught the slanting rays of the setting sun. Probably Mr. Pellitier and Mr. LaFonde heading for their truck to drive to Canada with the puppies, Hannah thought sadly.

Near the shore of Beaver Island, in a clearing partly overgrown with scrub pine trees, Hannah spied an old farmhouse with its windows boarded up. Next to the house stood an old barn, a gaping hole in its roof where the boards had rotted, causing a cave-in. Hannah had seen this abandoned farmstead once before, when she and Mama had come here to pick berries. "Perhaps Papa will buy that old farm when we have money enough," Mama said that day. "He could repair the house and have more rooms to rent to tourists."

Far off, Beaver Lodge stood like a beautiful dollhouse beside the lake. What a lovely place we have to live in here on the lake, Hannah thought, looking at her handsome copper-roofed home built of logs. And it's not *that* far. I can still get home before dark if I hurry through the woods.

Soon Hannah rounded a clump of scrub pines

halfway down Bald Hill, on the side toward home. She could not see Beaver Lodge, but she didn't mind. The forest ahead was of majestic white pines, with sunlight filtering prettily through green needles from far above. It was an easy walk across a carpet of dry pine needles with clumps of spring violets here and there. As long as she kept her right shoulder toward the setting sun to the west, Hannah knew she would be walking south, straight toward the open pasture behind Papa's barn. Mama had taught her this when they had gone berrying together.

Hannah scurried along through the woods on smooth ground. But now the sun had set, and yet she felt sure she'd reach the open pasture at any moment.

What was that? A blowing and snuffing noise came from a thicket of underbrush just ahead. Hannah froze in her tracks. She knew Papa had said that there had been no bears seen on Beaver Island for many years. But bears could swim, couldn't they? And they *could* come back, couldn't they? The *Gazette* Mama bought in Laketon on her weekly shopping trip said a man had shot a black bear near Moosehead Lake just last week!

Hannah inched backwards, keeping her eyes glued to the thick bushes where she'd heard the noise. A dry branch snapped loudly beneath her sneaker. Suddenly a huge black shape rose from the middle of the brush. It snuffed madly. The creature whirled crazily, then bounded away in the darkness. Was the angry thumping in her ears the beast racing off—or her heart pounding? Hannah was not sure.

As fast as her wiry legs would go, Hannah raced

in the opposite direction. Wild raspberry bushes tore her shins with sharp thorns. Twice, a tree limb, which she had not seen in the dark, swatted her face, drawing blood.

Before she knew it, Hannah was over her sneakers in gooey muck. She realized she was in Juniper Bog. But she had no idea which way to high ground.

She stopped, catching her breath. The stars were coming out, and the thin light they gave outlined the trees. These were not the sturdy pines of the woods behind Papa's pasture. They were the spindly junipers that grew on the mucky bog. In her terror in the dark Hannah hadn't noticed that she'd left the pines and entered the smaller trees.

Ahead of her, the low puckerbrush of the open bog shimmered in the starlight. Far, far across the soggy ground, the silver thread of Bog Stream glimmered in the light of the rising moon. The stream wound away in the distance, where it disappeared into the forest at the edge of the bog. Worse, Hannah had no idea which way was home. She was not afraid in the woods in daylight, but Hannah could only guess what kind of creatures and terrors lurked on a nighttime bog.

"Dear Jesus," Hannah prayed aloud. "Help me get home, even if it takes all night. And don't let me panic!" No sooner had she prayed than an idea popped into her head: *Follow the stream.* Of course! The stream would lead to the lake, and no matter which way she walked, the shoreline around the island would lead her to the dock in front of Beaver Lodge. 'Even if it takes all night.' I wish I hadn't prayed that part of the prayer, she thought. Hannah slapped a mosquito on her cheek as she plodded along. The mosquitoes were a nasty nuisance, but she was confident now, no longer afraid.

Once, Hannah tripped over a rotten, moss-covered log. She landed facedown in the mud up to her elbows. Her hair was plastered with goo, and her tee shirt was caked with wet clay. But never mind. At least the mosquitoes weren't biting through the clay. Not so much, anyway. Hannah remembered reading in a book that early pioneers put mud poultices on insect bites. *Gross!* she had thought then. Now she was glad for the mud and clay.

Something solid loomed ahead in the darkness, and the silvery stream slid out of sight beneath it. A bridge? Where there's a bridge, there's a road. But where does the road go?

The bridge was built of rough logs, and Hannah scrambled up it on bruised knees. The road under her sneakers, Hannah discovered as she trudged along, was made of logs like the bridge. Then it dawned on her. She was following Papa's corduroy road straight toward home!

"Putt-putt-putt-putt-cough-putt-putt-putt!" Hannah could not mistake that sound. Papa's old green John Deere tractor bounced toward her from the forest up ahead, the yellow gleam of its head-lights flickering through the night air. Another light, more powerful than the headlamps, played back and forth across the soggy bog. Papa was driving the tractor, and Mama, bouncing behind on the tractor's drawbar, was searching for Hannah with Papa's powerful spotlight.

"Mama! Papa! It's me! Here I am!" Hannah waved her arms above her head as she ran. Then she stopped, blinded as Mama turned the spotlight square into her eyes.

"The men—they took all three puppies," Hannah shouted.

"We know, baby. You look a sight!"

Usually it made Hannah mad when Mama called her 'baby.' Tonight Hannah did not mind, as Mama folded her, mud, mosquito bites and all, against her soft flannel shirt.

Chapter Four

Lace and Leather

"It could have been a bear, couldn't it?" Hannah ignored Walt as he rudely mimicked the remark she had made the evening before when she had told Mama and Papa why she'd run onto the bog although she was almost home.

"Yes, Walter, it *could* have been a bear—or perhaps a big buck deer or a bull moose," Mama said, defending Hannah. "Now hurry off to the barn and help Papa get ready to build fences. He may even let you drive the tractor."

Hannah rolled her eyes and swished the last drop of water from a plate with a dish towel. "What makes boys like that, Mama?"

"Perhaps he feels his masculinity threatened," Mama chuckled, though her eyes looked worried. "Treat him nice. He'll come around one of these days."

"Well, I'm glad it was only Ebony and not a bear," Hannah sighed. "After Papa bought Ebony for a driving horse last week, he said he'd teach me how to drive him."

"Did he say he'd teach Walter to drive Ebony, too?"

"Oh, yes." Hannah tossed her blonde braid, as she reached for the cupboard shelf to put away a mixing bowl. "But Papa told Walt to rein his horses in a bit. Walt gets to drive the tractor or the motorboat alone most anytime Papa needs him to run an errand. Papa doesn't think I'm ready to drive machines by myself yet. He says I may get to learn to handle Ebony *first*." Hannah's eyes shone with glee, and she chuckled as she spoke.

"Sounds fair to me," Mama agreed. "I just hope you don't go gloating around your big brother."

❋ ❋ ❋ ❋ ❋ ❋ ❋

"Puppies chew, kittens mew;
Rats gnaw, crows caw;
Crickets creak and mousies squeak.
Puppies chew . . . "

Hannah stopped in the middle of her rhyming to pick up one of Walt's L. L. Bean boots from the back hall. Hunter, his long legs at an ungainly gallop, tumbled from a dark corner where he'd been napping and scurried rattlite for the kitchen door.

Hannah held the boot up to catch the afternoon sun streaming down the hall. She had been helping Mama clean the old lodge, readying it for paying summer guests who would start arriving next week. She noticed that Hunter was not in the old wooden box he'd shared with Missy behind the kitchen's wood-fired range. He was not in the living room, either, where he sometimes curled up in the sun on the braided rug.

Hannah checked upstairs. Only yesterday

Hunter had managed to hop the steps as far as the landing, but his low-bellied basset mother, Missy, couldn't follow him. What piteous howls the two hounds had raised—Hunter, too terrified to climb back down and fat, short-legged Missy, unable to rescue her growing pup!

Then Hannah noticed that the door into the back hall, used only for hanging winter clothes or storing cleaning supplies, was ajar. Sure enough, Hunter had scurried in there, then bumped the door almost shut, so he was trapped.

In disgust, Hannah picked up a leather-topped boot from where she was sure Walt had thrown it on the hall floor. Then she turned it over.

Hannah felt her stomach churn as she first glanced at the boot's mate, neatly in its place on the rubber mat, and then back at the one she held. The expensive boot's leather tongue had been completely chewed off!

She remembered in dismay how Walt had saved for months from his allowance to buy the boots last fall. True, he'd had a growth spurt during the winter, so that he could no longer wear the boots with two pairs of wool socks. But with summer coming on, Walt still wore them on rainy days with thin socks.

Right after lunch, Hannah showed Walt the ruined boot. "I'm sorry, Walt. I must've left the hall door unlatched when I put Mama's mop away. I'll make up for it," she apologized.

"Those boots cost me eighty bucks," Walt roared. "What can *you* do to replace 'em! And I was goin' t' give 'em to you this fall. Now nobody has boots!" He hurled the boot through the hall door and raced off toward the barn.

"It's just as well your father didn't see that," Mama said softly.

Hannah, angry beyond tears, was silent for a moment. "I guess I'd be pretty mad if *my* stuff got torn up," she sighed at last. "But Walt's got no right to act so mean."

That evening Hannah peeked into an old metal cookie tin in which she kept special things. There, wrapped in moss, was a rough pearl she'd pried from a freshwater clam along the lakeshore. In a velvet case with a snap lid was Grandma Parmenter's wedding ring, which Grandma had given Hannah just before she died. Very special, too, were two locks of blonde hair—one taken from Grandma's head as a small girl, and the other cut from Hannah's own baby curls. It gave Hannah goose bumps to realize that had she not labeled the locks she wouldn't be able to tell which was hers and which was Grandma's.

Hannah picked up a brown envelope tied with a string. She squeezed it, thinking of the rare occasions when Mama took her to the mall in Skowhegan. Hannah would raid her precious hoard—money saved from her allowance, tips from guests when she served meals, cash from selling Christmas wreaths in Laketon—and she would take out a five or a ten to buy herself something nice. Tonight Hannah opened the envelope. She slid out a corner of a bill, just enough to see that it was a twenty.

"How much d'you figure your boots were worth, big brother—before Hunter chewed 'em, that is?" Hannah asked next morning at breakfast.

"Why is that important to you?" Hannah knew that Walt's answer was intended to intimidate, and she remained silent.

"Your sister asked a fair question, Walt," Papa intoned sternly.

Walt shrugged. "Twenty dollars. I'd pretty much outgrown 'em. But they *were* in good shape."

"Will you sell them for that?" Hannah inquired.

"I suppose." Walt eyed her suspiciously.

"Now, see here," interrupted Mama. "Hannah's not obliged to pay Walter for an old pair of boots he's outgrown!"

"Sandy," Papa gently intervened. "Hannah is almost a woman. I expect she should make her own decision."

Later that morning, Mama excused her daughter from helping with the house chores when Hannah explained that it was time Hunter had a home. "At least until he outgrows his chewing stage," said Hannah.

Hannah crawled beneath the porch into the space that had been Missy's house until the puppies were born. It was a cozy spot, worn smooth by long doggie use and littered with an old blanket, two old coats, and a lot of straw from the barn.

Missy's hole had no walls, since it was open clear to the house foundation. Hannah raided Papa's board pile beside the barn. She dragged out two old doors and an armload of boards Papa had thrown out when he'd built a stall for Ebony. Then Hannah found Papa's hammer, a saw, and a can of nails in the garage.

"There!" Hannah exclaimed, after she had pounded for more than two hours. "Perfect home for a hound."

Mama, who had come out to inspect Hannah's work, agreed that it looked fine. "But you've got to have a chain," Mama observed.

"Chain?" Hannah was worried.

"Puppies like to explore. We can't be searching the woods for Hunter every night. He'll need to be tied until he learns where his home is."

Hannah remembered the old dog chain and collar the former owners of Beaver Lodge had left hanging on a nail in the woodshed. That evening she tied Hunter to the porch, then pushed him inside his new home with Missy.

Late that night, Hannah watched the moon set over Mt. Kineo, far down Moosehead Lake. She had waked up half an hour earlier, and unable to sleep, she curled up in the old armchair by her bedroom window. 'Almost a woman,' Papa had said. It gave Hannah shivers just to remember it. Mama might have said the same thing, but to hear Papa use those words gave Hannah a thrill deep in her soul. Will I ever understand myself? she thought.

She eyed the Bean boots next to her bed. They were hers now, and Papa had promised to repair the tongue Hunter had chewed with rivets and a scrap of leather.

Outside, Hannah could hear Hunter's pathetic whine. She decided she wouldn't be able to sleep until he quieted down. Softly slipping downstairs in her bare feet, Hannah stole outside and gathered Hunter into her arms.

Hannah was careful to place her sneakers and boots on her dresser out of Hunter's reach before she crawled back into bed. She snuggled Hunter against her, keeping the sheet between them, before pulling the blanket over them both.

With the first rays of dawn, Hannah rolled over and reached for the warm, breathing lump that had lain against her for hours, helping her fall asleep.

Hunter was gone! Hannah sat up, but her bedroom door was still tightly closed.

"You rascal!" Hannah cried, spying her pup asleep in her easy chair.

Mama was expecting guests that day, and she had reminded Hannah to dress extra nice. Hannah whistled as she fished the flowered skirt Aunt Theresa Boudreau had bought her in Laketon from her closet. She looked for her new sweatshirt, which she'd left on the back of her chair. The shirt was a dreamy robin's egg blue, with cute teddy bears hugging each other across the front. The bears were framed in lace, and the shirt's neck and cuffs also had lace.

Hannah found the sweatshirt rumpled under Hunter. She tugged it out, then her mouth fell open. Hunter's languid brown eyes met Hannah's angry blue ones. Half a yard of nylon lace had not even given him a bellyache.

"You dirty dog! You nasty, nasty puppy!" She swatted Hunter with the sweatshirt, but he only leaped to the floor and trotted halfway to the door. Hunter wrinkled a puzzled eyebrow and looked back sorrowfully.

Hannah sat on her bed and sobbed. Then she remembered Walt's wrath over the Bean boots, and she began to laugh.

Chapter Five

A Dog's Day

Hannah loved misty Maine summer mornings in her island home. Though the calendar in the kitchen of Beaver Lodge said that sunrise came shortly after four a.m., it was often mid-morning before the sun came out in its glory as the fog lifted and she could see Mt. Kineo far down Moosehead Lake, the other lake islands, and Laketon on the mainland.

"Good boy," she murmured, scratching Hunter behind each floppy ear, then letting him nuzzle his wet nose against her shin as she reached for a boot from her perch on the porch steps. The Bean boots were Hannah's now, and she liked to wear them in the early morning until the dew dried off the wet grass and she changed to sneakers for the rest of the day.

Mama and Papa, Hannah knew, would not be up until five o'clock—Walt a little later. The six vacationing "guests" might roll out at seven, in time for Mama and Hannah to serve them a breakfast of blueberry pancakes and bacon in the dining room.

But for now, the world of Beaver Island was Hannah's alone—hers and Hunter's to savor and enjoy.

"Stop that!" Hannah batted Hunter's nose. The pup was chewing on one boot's leather lace as she tied the other. Hannah scooted away, letting Hunter stretch to the end of his chain trying to reach her. She giggled as her hound trembled with excitement, his ratty tail wagging as though it would surely snap off. She tied her other lace, then bent to set him free.

"Back off, feller," Hannah exclaimed, trying to unsnap his chain. Finally she picked up her struggling pup, then, his chain off, she dropped him. Hunter shot away, disappearing in the fog toward Papa's barn.

Hannah hurried toward the pasture on the hillside above the barn. Hunter reappeared from the fog, circled his mistress gleefully, then bounded away, following his delicate nose. Seconds later, he trotted back, whimpering in disappointment.

"Tried to catch a mousie, did y', boy?" Hannah laughed. "Or was it a rabbit? Mice and rabbits have holes, and you'll have to be quicker'n that if you're going to live up to your name!"

They arrived at the pasture gate made of cedar rails set into a fence of barbed wire. Far, far up the hill, where the rocky pasture sloped towards the forest and Bald Hill, Hannah could just see the tops of a row of black spruces intermingled with towering pines that caught the sun above the ground fog. Just beyond these was the woods where she'd gotten lost, though nearly home, Hannah now knew.

Hannah climbed the cedar gate bars, swinging one limber leg across, then whistled. A thumping along the ground near the woods caught her ear, and she whistled again. This time the noise grew to a rumble, like the thundering that had frightened her the evening she had walked home alone after leaving the puppies with the Canadien woodchoppers.

"Here, boy," Hannah cried. Galloping out of the mist, Ebony appeared, his sleek black coat glistening with nighttime dew, his eyes alight with expectation. Hannah fished into the pocket of her light denim jacket and produced a handful of sugar cubes she had taken from the dining room bowl. Ebony drew his black lips back into a silly horsey grin, then nuzzled her hand as he lapped up the treat.

"You'n I are gonna ride like the wind one o' these days, big guy! Then we can go places on this island where you can't haul that ol' wagon," Hannah cried. She patted Ebony's nose, and he trotted off in search of clover.

Hannah, perched on the rail, felt fortunate indeed to be mistress not only to a hound but also to this fine stallion. Papa hadn't given Ebony to her, exactly, but he was more and more trusting Ebony into Hannah's care. When Papa sees I can care for Hunter, Hannah told herself, perhaps he'll make Ebony my responsibility, too.

Before Hannah's eyes, Molly seemed to materialize, her cream-colored coat so blending with the fog that she was all but invisible until she reached the gate. Molly lowed in expectation, and Hannah could see by the cow's plump udder that she needed Walt's attention in the barn right soon.

A brown, fuzzy creature appeared behind Molly, its tough, stubby horns just barely sticking up through the fur on its knobby head. The animal reached its snout beneath Molly for a drink of milk. But Molly kicked, and "Ufff!" the hungry critter backed off.

"That'll teach y', Bullet!" Hannah chortled. But Bullet, Molly's spring bull calf, tried again for a swig. This time his mother, who seemed to know that her milk was needed at Beaver Lodge for breakfast, turned on her son with her one crumpled horn. Molly butted Bullet soundly, as Hannah yelled, "Behave yourself, you rascal!"

Bullet backed away, and he stood so sorrowful and lonesome in the mist that Hannah felt sorry for the calf—almost.

"Rrrruff!" It was Hunter, and he seemed determined to finish what Molly had begun. Straight for Bullet's ankles Hunter raced, snapping and yipping as he bounded along. Young hound and young calf disappeared into the fog. Hannah could hear Bullet's hooves pounding as, "Yip, yip, yip," Hunter raced after him across the pasture.

"Hunter! Come back! That's enough! Hunter!"

Hunter did not obey.

"Hunter!"

The thunder of tiny hooves and excited yipping continued.

Then—"Ike, ike, ike!"

"Baw-w-w!"

"Ike, ike, ike!"

Hannah froze on her perch on the gate bars for only an instant longer. Then, remembering Bullet's stubby but useful horns, she grabbed the stick Walt used to guide Molly into the barn and raced across the pasture.

Hannah had once seen a dogfight between two strays in Laketon, but this fight both frightened and

surprised her. Fangs and horns, paws and hooves—
it was not an even match.

Bullet's shins were bloody from Hunter's bites,
but Hunter, covered with his own blood, was clearly
getting the worst of it.

"Hunter!" Hannah screamed, spotting her half-
grown hound shivering in the corner of the pasture.

Bullet lowered his head and charged. Hunter the
brave stood his ground. As Bullet closed in, Hunter
dodged, diving for the calf's throat.

Bullet dodged, too, and he caught the flying dog
squarely in the ribs. Hannah watched in dismay
and disbelief as Bullet lifted Hunter on his horns,
tossing him perhaps ten feet closer to the fence.
Hunter scrambled to his feet as Bullet circled for
another charge.

What happened next surprised Hannah so
much that weeks afterward, she and Mama were
still trying to figure it out. Hannah loved Hunter,
but she was fond of Bullet, too. She still remembered him as a trembling newborn calf in the early
spring, on unsteady legs, his fur being licked down
by mother Molly's wet, loving tongue. For weeks,
until Papa had put Bullet out to pasture, Hannah
had carded him daily to keep his woolly coat sleek,
then laughed in glee as he ate his calf grain out of
her fingers, tickling them with his tough bovine
tongue to get the last of the sticky molasses from
her hands.

"Bullet! Stop!" Hannah now yelled. They had
been the best of friends when he was a hornless calf
penned up in Papa's barn, and she expected him to
obey her.

But Bullet was a jersey bull. He dropped his hot
little head, fire in his eyes. His hooves set up an

angry clatter on the rocky hillside pasture. He charged—straight for Hannah!

Hannah suddenly remembered Hunter's bloody coat, and she decided that she'd rather not have one like it. She flattened out and rolled clear of Bullet's horns. As the young bull sailed past, Hannah saw Hunter disappear through the barbed wire where Bullet could not follow.

Bullet was between her and the gate, circling for another attack. Hannah quickly decided she preferred barbed wire to his well-aimed horns.

❋ ❋ ❋ ❋ ❋ ❋ ❋

Mama carefully checked the bones of each puppy leg as Hunter lay across Hannah's knees in the kitchen. Mama set him on the floor on all fours, and he took a few limping steps, punctuating each movement with a piteous cry of "Ike!"

Mama picked Hunter up and passed him to Hannah.

"What do you think, Mama?"

"He'll live," Mama dryly replied. "That's quite a rip in your denim jacket, though. Did Bullet do that?"

"I...I don't think so," Hannah said, embarrassed, remembering the barbed-wire fence. She felt Hunter's ribcage. As she found a soft spot, Hunter screamed "IKE!" and snapped at her hand.

"Broken rib?" Hannah asked.

"Sure is," Mama agreed. "That's his lesson about livestock. It's just as well he learned while he's still a puppy. And it could as easily have been *your* rib," Mama added darkly.

"What can we do?"

Mama ran her fingers lovingly through Hannah's hair. "You can put Hunter back behind the stove until he heals, I guess. But you *must* keep him tied to the stove leg," Mama added, with a worried nod toward the living room where two new, leather-upholstered chairs stood for the use of paying guests.

"I love you dearly, Hunter," Hannah cooed, gently placing him on an old blanket behind the wood stove, which was not used in summer except in the early morning. She helped him find a comfortable position in which to lie, then hurried into the bathroom in search of a hot water bottle.

Hannah later found Bullet in the barn, where Papa was scrubbing the calf's injuries with peroxide while Walt hung onto the protesting beast's halter.

"Your dog really messed Bullet up," grumbled Walt. He braced his feet to keep Bullet's head down while Papa doctored him, and said no more.

"Just scratched his skin a bit," Papa chuckled, trying to smooth things over. "I'm sure Hunter didn't hurt the bull inside a bit."

"Well, I'm glad of that," Hannah said, relieved. "Though I'm afraid it's my fault for not keeping Hunter out of the pasture. But Bullet sure tried to hurt the girl inside, I guess." She rubbed a sore shoulder where she'd rolled onto a rock to escape Bullet's horns. "And it's not been a good day for a dog, either."

"Are you having one of those days when you need to go back to bed and get up on the other side?" Papa laughed. "Well, we're keeping Bullet hitched in a stall from now on. He's getting too big to run free. Bulls can be dangerous, and a jersey bull is the most nervous beast of all."

Chapter Six

Bones and Broken Promises

"Fish and dogs don't mix," warned Mama mildly as Hannah cleared the supper table. The three couples who were guests for a week at Beaver Lodge had finished eating and strolled onto the screened porch to watch the sun set over Moosehead Lake. Mama had fried a batch of perch and pickerel caught by one of the men the evening before. A large dish of fish bones sat with some other table scraps to feed Mama's dozen Rhode Island Red hens.

"I won't let Hunter near them, Mama," Hannah promised. To tell the truth, it peeved Hannah to hear Mama remind her to watch what she fed Hunter. Hannah had nursed her pup back to health after Bullet the bull calf had tossed him with his stubby horns, so she felt very competent at caring for dogs.

"C'mon, boy!" Hannah unhitched Hunter's chain, and she let him jump and leap at her for a few seconds while she petted him with her free hand, holding the bowl of table scraps with the other.

"Down!" she commanded. Hunter obediently returned to all fours, trotting at Hannah's side, his long, intelligent head—part of his Labrador heritage—held high as they hurried toward the hen yard.

Hunter seemed to sense that the hens, not he, were about to be fed the tantalizing fish scraps. Whining and dancing around hungrily, he fairly shook with excitement as Hannah threw the bowl's contents at the greedy hens.

"Yipe!" Hunter got too close to the battery-powered electric wire Papa had installed outside the hen yard to keep skunks, coons, and even Hunter from helping themselves to the eggs or to a fat hen.

"Stings, huh?" laughed Hannah. She knew from experience that Papa's electric fences, though harmless, were unpleasant to tangle with. "Guess you'll learn better soon enough," she chuckled as, tail tucked in, Hunter flew down the path and disappeared into his home under the porch.

Hannah opened a Tupperware dish of stuff Mama said had been in the refrigerator too long, and she was about to hurl its contents at the poultry. "What's this?" It was pork steak, still fairly fresh. Remembering poor Hunter's disappointment at seeing the hens get his dessert, she saved it.

Hannah sat on the porch steps for a moment after feeding the chickens. She knew she had to chain Hunter to keep him from roaming the nighttime forest, and she felt pity for his having to learn all his lessons the hard way.

"C'm here, Hunt," she called, whistling.

Hunter crept outside. He eyed his mistress sorrowfully.

"Here you go!" She held the pork steak out.

Hunter snatched it from her hand without so much as an "arf" in thanks.

"Uff-ulp," and down it went.

"Pig!" Hannah teased.

Hunter danced around her, his happy spirits returning.

Hannah collared her hound, then snapped the brass catch on his chain in place.

"*Where* did you learn your table manners?" she exclaimed. "No wonder Mama's afraid you'll eat the fish, bones and all!"

She kissed his nose, then hurried indoors to help Mama finish the evening's kitchen chores.

A few evenings later, Papa's paying guests were playing Monopoly at the porch table, though Papa had reminded them that it was a good night for fishing.

"These city tourists," he whispered to Mama and Hannah in the kitchen. "They'll fish all day in the hot sun and catch nothing. The Lord gives us a south wind in the evening, but they want to play board games!"

"When the wind is from the south,
It blows the hook in fishes' mouth,"

Mama quoted, chuckling.

"Since none of the guests want it tonight, may I use the canoe to fish for catfish?" Hannah inquired of her father.

Mama shot a worried glance at Papa.

"Hannah's responsible," Papa said firmly. "And she's a good swimmer."

"Be sure you wear your life jacket," Mama admonished. "And stay in sight of the lodge. If I can't see Papa's gas lantern shining from the canoe, we're coming to find you in the motorboat!"

"I promise," Hannah agreed.

Papa had bought an expensive Old Town canoe for his guests' use, and he hadn't even let Walt take it out alone. This will be a real treat, Hannah thought, as she eased the canoe out of the boathouse, careful not to drag it over any rocks. She tied Hunter to the front seat so he wouldn't knock over the lantern, then placed her bamboo cane pole and a can of worms for catfish bait in the middle of the canoe.

Next, Hannah sprayed her face, hands, and ankles with insect repellent. She knew what Papa meant when he joked, "A fisherman is just another link in the food chain. Feed the fish worms while the mosquitoes eat you. And last of all you eat the fish."

"If I had fur like you, Hunter, I wouldn't need this nasty ol' stuff," Hannah chuckled grimly.

"Arf!" Hunter merrily agreed. Even though it was a cloudy, starless night, Hannah easily found the point of land that hid the marshy cove where the catfish fed among the pond lilies. She paddled around the point and into a spot where the lily pads gently held the canoe from drifting. Then she lighted the lantern to save her flashlight batteries, adjusting it until it glowed brightly. She held it up for a moment as she peered across the treeless point of land, over which she could just make out the outline of Beaver Lodge's second story.

The yellow glow of a kerosene lamp appeared in the upstairs hall window, then vanished. "Good old Mama," Hannah remarked to Hunter. "She's checking up on me. Doesn't she know I'm 'most an adult?"

Hannah cast her line into the murky marsh

water, and the bobber disappeared almost as soon as the hook sank. She set the hook, then hauled it in. Her bamboo pole was without a reel, better for catfish fishing than a flyrod, since Hannah didn't need to wind the line in with each catch.

The fish was an ugly flatfish, tough and scaly. Hannah worked her hook loose, then threw the bristly creature back.

"Yuck!"

"R-r-rugg!" agreed Hunter.

Three casts in a row brought in three nice catfish. Then she caught a flatfish. She noticed its hook injury from before.

"Same one—you're a slow learner!" This time Hannah tossed the flatfish behind her, splashing it among the lily pads and cattails.

An hour's fishing gave Hannah a bucket of small catfish, known in Maine as horned pout. The flatfish, which had been her first fish of the evening, persisted in getting itself onto her hook a third time.

"You like my hook?" Hannah sarcastically remarked. "Well, you can stay, then!" She tossed it into the bottom of the canoe beyond the lantern, but just out of Hunter's reach, where it lay still. Hunter sniffed at it hungrily, then whimpered and complained, making a regular nuisance of himself for the rest of the evening.

Intent on her sport, Hannah ignored Hunter. At last she dumped the rest of her worms overboard, then held the lantern over the water, watching the fish grab them as they sank.

Hannah rinsed the dirt out of her worm can. Then she ladled lake water into her bucket to keep her catfish submerged.

From her jacket pocket Hannah fished an old,

bone-handled knife. It had once been a butcher knife, but the blade had worn, then snapped off. Papa had reground it to make an all-purpose tool, handy for digging out fishhooks and other tough jobs.

Hannah cut a dozen of the best water lilies she could find, plopping them into the bucket on top of her fish. They'd be beautiful floating in a glass bowl on the dining room table, she decided.

Hannah's hound suddenly sprang into action. The flatfish had flipped within his reach.

"Hunter, no!" she cried. Hannah dived for her dog, nearly capsizing the canoe. She twisted his collar until he almost strangled, then pried the fish from his fangs.

"Naughty, naughty pup!" Hannah sat down, panting, clutching the mangled flatfish. Then she laughed. "You don't understand, do you, boy?"

Hannah stared at the fish. Mama had once fed Hunter a boneless fish fillet. *Why not?* With the old knife, Hannah quickly removed the head and tail, then filleted the flatfish. She tossed the backbone into the marsh. Then Hannah tossed Hunter the fish flesh. She laughed in glee as he wolfed it down.

❄ ❄ ❄ ❄ ❄ ❄ ❄

"Your dog is looking rather peaked," Papa remarked a couple of days after Hannah and Hunter's fishing trip.

"You think he's ill, Papa?"

Hannah was helping Mama get dinner ready as Papa returned from a canoe trip up the brook of Juniper Bog with a couple of guests.

"He *hasn't* shown much interest in following me

around today. Maybe he caught something in that damp night air when I took him fishing with me."

"Oh?" Papa was surprised. "I thought he was asleep under the porch all that night."

Chapter Seven

A–Hunting
We Will Go

"Mama, I wish you'd let me use my calculator for math."

Hannah pushed herself away from the school desk Papa had installed next to the dining room window to help her and Walt get into a proper scholarly attitude for their home-schooling sessions.

"When we start algebra you may use a calculator—not before. That's two years away," Mama said firmly.

"Aww, I used one when I helped you figure prof it and loss on the tourist operation this summer. So did you." Hannah smiled brightly, hoping friendly persuasion would help Mama see her inconsistency.

"Give me the decimal equivalent of one sixteenth. Do the math in your head."

"I *know* the formula, Mama. You divide the denominator into the numerator. That's what's important, right?"

"Agreed. But until you can recognize basic com-putations instantly in your head, you're a slave to anyone who can do so. Now that's final."

"We-l-ll, all right. Can you check my work?"

Hannah knew that Mama was right, and she was just a mite ashamed for pushing the issue. But an hour changing endless proper and improper fractions into decimals and percentages had left her feeling a bit sorry for herself. She passed her papers to her mother.

"Perfect, as usual," Mama remarked moments later. "Guess you've got a couple of hours you can call your own."

"I'm taking Hunter into the woods, Mama—that is, if you don't mind."

"Have a good time," Mama laughed. "Might as well get your hiking done now. Come hunting sea-son, you'll need to stay close to home because Papa will be out there with deer hunters from the city. He tries to teach them better, but some of those fellows will shoot at anything that moves."

"We're going around Bald Hill. I'm teaching Hunter to hunt."

"With a gun?" Mama was alarmed.

"No, Mama. I'm not even taking Walt's slingshot. I said hunt, not kill," she emphasized. "We're just goin' t' find us some animals."

"Well, be *sure* you carry a compass. We certainly don't need any more nighttime search parties!"

Mama is a worrywart, Hannah thought, as she pulled on her new wool sweater. But as Mama once said, 'Someone around here's got to be concerned about things.' Hannah knew that carrying a com-pass in the woods is only common sense.

Besides, Hannah sadly remembered Hunter's

bout with the bone from the flatfish she'd let him eat—her own foolishness in forgetting Mama's advice. The anxious trip to the veterinarian in Laketon to remove the fishbone lodged in his throat had cost her nearly all her savings.

"*What* have you killed this time?" Hannah found Walt outside with Hunter, Papa's shotgun cradled in his arm as he teased her hound with a limp, furry gray animal that he dangled by the tail.

Hunter strained at his chain, his nose atwitch, his legs trembling, his tail furiously wagging. Whatever Walt had shot, Hunter wanted it for a mid-afternoon snack.

"Can't have my gray squirrel, boy," Walter laughed. "I'm eating it for supper."

"Gross!"

"So? You catch fish and eat 'em. What's the difference?"

"But that's such a beautiful creature!" Hannah protested.

"So was the deer Papa shot last fall. But I noticed you ate the steaks and hamburg he made from it without complaining!"

"You're right," Hannah sighed. She'd lost two battles in a row, and she knew better than to argue further.

But Hunter, Hannah knew, would love her unconditionally. No arguments. Never a disagreement. Even if she'd been mean to him, Hunter would come to nuzzle her or follow her around Papa's farm, his warm eyes adoring Hannah's every move.

"C'mon, boy." Hannah unhitched Hunter's chain. "Walt can have his silly old squirrel. You and I are goin' hunting ourselves."

Hunter scampered across the field behind the house, his nose to the ground, following a zigzag trail Hannah guessed had been made by a rabbit. He reached the edge of a field Papa had plowed a few days earlier, so he could plant corn in the spring. Hunter stopped, circled back, then returned to the field. He sat down and whined, puzzled.

Hannah soon caught up with Hunter, and *her* nose told her at once what was confusing her pup's sensitive nostrils. Papa had been spreading cow manure on the field that morning. The rabbit, which must have crossed the field just before Papa went out with his tractor, could no longer be tracked by scent. Though Hannah easily found bunny tracks in the freshly tilled soil, Hunter refused to follow them. Eyesight and common sense aside, Hunter merely circled back on a trail that led nowhere.

So Hannah fished a ball of heavy hay-binder twine from her pocket. She tied it to Hunter's collar and led him across the field. But when scent contradicted sense, Hunter resisted, and he complained all the way.

Hannah found where the rabbit tracks had left the tilled field and entered grass once again. Hunter found the spot, too, for his nose caught the scent, and he tore off, Hannah racing behind.

Hunter's hunt ended beside the woods, where an old stone wall covered with blackberry brambles provided protection for the rabbit's hole. Hunter at once began to dig with all his might, but he soon ran into stones. Excitement overran sense, and Hunter whimpered and trembled in frustration at not being able to dig the rabbit out.

"We can hunt, you'n me," Hannah laughed,

watching her silly hound dig and scratch at the stones. "Game's up. Now come along." She untied his twine leash, and he followed her along the wall to where Papa's road led into the woods.

Half an hour's tramp brought Hannah and Hunter to the path leading off the tractor road and up to the blueberry barrens on Bald Hill. Hunter hurried ahead. Hannah whistled, and her dog waited obediently. Then Hunter spotted a grasshopper on a stalk of goldenrod that bent over the path. Hannah laughed in glee as Hunter's doggie instinct took over. The long-legged insect was quick, but Hunter was quicker. He caught the hapless creature in midair and gulped it down.

A quarter mile up the path, Hunter's nose lifted. He danced in a circle for a moment, then plunged into the underbrush. Hannah was not ready for this.

"Hunter, come back, boy!" she called. "Come back here!"

But Hunter ignored her, and he raced on, baying happily at whatever it was that had caught his nostrils. The trail zigzagged, so running in a straight line, Hannah kept him in sight.

Soon she found him beneath an old, hollow beech tree, barking indignantly at a red squirrel, much smaller than the gray one Walt had brought home. And the sassy squirrel was scolding right back from his perch out of Hunter's reach!

Hannah laughed as though her sides would split at the silly scene. The squirrel seemed to realize that Hunter could not climb. It kept up an angry chatter, which Hannah found as funny as Hunter's complaints.

But the chase seemed to be over. So Hannah

tossed a stick at the squirrel, and a crimson streak tore down a long branch of the beech, then leaped onto the ground.

Hunter was off again, and he refused to wait for Hannah. Hannah raced over the top of Bald Hill, only to see her hound tearing down the other side, hard on the heels of the small red creature. She ran after him, but the red squirrel disappeared into the branches of a spruce growing up from the bottom of a low cliff.

"Here, boy—heel!" Hannah panted. Hunter sat on his haunches at the edge of the cliff, above the tree. Hannah grabbed for his collar—too late! The squirrel appeared on a branch just below Hannah and her hound, and Hunter leaped down onto the tree at once.

Hunter landed thrashing and clawing among the spruce tree's limbs, and he hung on for his life. He was stranded, since the limber branches would give him no foothold to spring back.

Hannah scrambled down over broken shale, dirt, and loose rocks until at last she reached the base of the cliff. The spruce towered above her, and poor Hunter, whimpering and crying, was stranded high up. The tiny red squirrel, which had tantalized him into this trap, was long gone.

Hannah was about to yank off the new wool cable-knit sweater that she'd worn over an old sweatshirt to protect her from the fall chill and start up the bristly, pitch-sticky branches. Then she heard Hunter yelp in terror, and it tore at her heart.

Still wearing her nice sweater, Hannah tackled a bottom branch, then boosted herself up. Spruce limbs grow close together, and she climbed easily enough. But the rough bark made her fingers raw, and she could feel the branches tearing at her sweater.

* * * * * * *

"It's a good thing you decided not to buy the *white* sweater," Mama told an unhappy Hannah that evening as mother and daughter checked out the sticky gray patches ground into the brown woolen sleeves. "I can get the pitch out with some of the white gasoline we use for Papa's lantern—I hope," Mama softly murmured. "But it will be slightly stained."

"At least my hands will heal," Hannah said sadly. "If only I hadn't thrown a stick at that red squirrel!"

"Remember, Hannah, there are no 'if onlies' with God," Mama smiled. "His Word, the Bible, tells us to forget those things that are behind and press on to the good things God has in store for us. We make mistakes—that's a part of life," Mama added. "But it's more important that we focus on our goals."

Chapter Eight

Hunting Hunter

"Mama, I could put only one bar of soap in each of the guest rooms 'cause I ran out."

"No harm done," chuckled Mama. "We're going shopping in Laketon tomorrow right after breakfast. I have to get a boatload of supplies before the bird hunters arrive."

"Tomorrow is Thursday," Hannah protested, remembering that she needed to spend each weekday morning on schoolwork.

"You're way ahead in most of your subjects. You could spend an extra hour studying Saturday," affirmed Mama. "Papa's going to need to help Walter with his studies while we're gone. But Papa and I knew there'd be days like this when we decided to live on this island and school you kids at home."

❋ ❋ ❋ ❋ ❋ ❋ ❋

The goldenrod along the path to the henhouse was white with frost the next morning at daybreak, but Hannah did not mind. She hurried toward the pen, where Rusty was welcoming the sun by crowing his crested head off from his perch atop the hanging feeder.

"Shoo! Go crow someplace else, you rascal!" Hannah cried, chasing Rusty off the feeder's post. Having an old red rooster known to peck and claw looking her in the eye as she worked made Hannah nervous.

Hannah filled the feeder with laying mash, then checked the nests after the hens came out to eat. Already half a dozen warm brown eggs, Hannah discovered, were ready for her family's breakfast.

❋ ❋ ❋ ❋ ❋ ❋ ❋

Mama settled into the prow of the motorboat, and Hunter leaped in after her.

"Hannah, you may drive the boat," she said. "Just be careful until we're clear of the point."

Hannah took the wheel of the outboard, which Papa had already started for her. Slowly, she opened the gas.

The big, open boat moved swiftly away from Beaver Lodge's dock. Hannah pointed it toward the lake, intending to circle toward Laketon as soon as they cleared the point.

A light mist over Moosehead Lake still veiled the mainland, and Hannah could not see Laketon. That was okay. Once the boat was well under way, she'd simply motor south by the boat's compass until she saw Laketon's only traffic signal blinking through the fog.

Suddenly a black shape loomed directly ahead. Hannah cut the gas and spun the wheel at the same time.

"Hey!" Mama yelled, grabbing her seat for balance as the boat careened.

"Ike! Arf," Hunter complained as he tumbled off his seat.

The boat shot past the black object—and Hannah discovered that it had four legs and massive antlers. A bull moose, water weeds dripping from its ugly snout, lumbered toward the point as the boat sped past, barely missing him. A mossy gray rock in the water just past the moose caused Hannah's blood to chill as she realized that had the Lord not put the big beast out there, they'd surely have crashed and sunk.

❋ ❋ ❋ ❋ ❋ ❋ ❋

"Hey, San-day!" Mama's brother-in-law, Uncle Joe Boudreau, met Hannah and Mama at the door that afternoon. Uncle Joe was French Canadien, and he still spoke with a strong French accent, especially when he pronounced Mama's name, Sandy.

"Brought y' little red wagon, I see," chuckled Mama's sister, Aunt Theresa. She nodded toward Hannah and Walt's old Radio Flyer wagon, its high wooden sides bursting with groceries from Northland Market.

"Well, it's not little, exactly," panted Hannah, who had been taking her turn pulling the wagon. The red wagon had never been 'little,' Hannah thought. As a little kids in Skowhegan, she remembered, she and Walt had easily fit into it together to coast into the gulley behind their house. How heavy even the empty wagon then seemed, when Walt ran on ahead and didn't help pull it. Now Hannah and

Mama had brought the red wagon to carry their purchases to the boat from the stores along Laketon's Main Street. Hunter, hitched behind on his chain, trotted along obediently.

"Won't you come in?" Aunt Theresa invited. "I've just made my first pie from my fall mincemeat. I'll drip us a pot of coffee."

"Can't wait for coffee, I'm afraid," Mama said with a worried glance at the black clouds rolling in from the west. "We'd best take our pie on paper plates and run."

"The lake, she has whitecaps, *non?*" Uncle Joe interrupted. "When ze ol' moose swish his tail, he's goin' to soon shake his antlers."

"Uncle Joe is right," Hannah agreed. The lake ,which had lain as smooth as silk beneath the fog at dawn, now had waves of foam. "I don't like the looks of it," she shivered, remembering foolish chances she had taken before.

"Why don't you eat with us?" Uncle Joe suggested. "Have some dinner. Ze storm, mebbe she pass by sundown, an' then you go home. Ze boat, she have a light, *non?*"

The rain did end by sunset, as Uncle Joe predicted. But the wind worsened, so that the windows of the Boudreaus' old house rattled and the house's timbers groaned. Faroff, peals of thunder could still be heard as darkness fell.

"Papa, we're safe at Uncle Joe and Aunt Theresa's. 10-4," Hannah spoke into the microphone of Uncle Joe's CB radio. Silence greeted her, except for static from the distant storm.

"Come in, Beaver Lodge. Do you read me?" she tried again. "10-4."

"This is Beaver Lodge, sweetheart," Papa's voice

crackled, finally. His next remark was lost in the static of the electrical storm, which had passed to the east.

"...sure glad to hear you're okay. 10-4."

"We're staying here tonight, Papa. 10-4."

"Gotcha!" Papa's voice came clearly this time. "Kiss Mama good night for me. 10-4."

"Will do," Hannah replied. "10-4."

※ ※ ※ ※ ※ ※ ※

"You've got to go out *again?*" Hannah crawled out of the sleeping bag on the glider where she'd been trying to fall asleep on the Boudreaus' back porch. Hunter, whimpering and insistent, had sprung to the floor from where he'd been sleeping across her feet. But Hannah had chained him to the glider, so he needed her attention to run outdoors. Sleepily, she undid his chain, then struggled out of the sleeping bag Aunt Theresa had given her to curl up in for the night. He scurried past her, butting the screen door with his nose and crowding through before she could open it. Soon he was back, and she let him in, leaving the screen door unfastened. No need to hitch it against mosquitoes this late in the fall; as for Hunter, she would chain him up, anyway.

A few hours later Hunter whimpered and strained at his chain. Hannah rolled over—it was not yet dawn.

"All right, all right! Guess you can let *yourself* out this time." She unsnapped his chain, and the rattle of the wooden screen door told her he was outside.

But Hunter was not keeping Hannah's feet

warm at dawn. Nor did she find him whining at the door. Ten minutes of tramping in the frosty grass outside the house in her bare feet was no use. Hunter did not answer her call.

Hannah yanked on her old Bean boots and ran to where she and Mama had left the boat at the public landing. No Hunter.

"We'll look for ze dog with ze car. We'll find him, sure," Uncle Joe promised. But though they drove down every street in the village and even out to several farms, no one had seen Hunter. He was now Hunter the hunted.

"Ze drug store, she have a photocopier," Uncle Joe suggested during breakfast. "Why not you make a poster an' copy it? Aunt Theresa and I, we'll put them all over town. I'll take some to Skowhegan next week, mebbe."

White hound with brown ears and brown saddle on back. Left ear deeply notched, Hannah wrote in large letters with a felt-tip marker. Her tears stained the paper as she worked, carefully lettering her sign. *Phone Joe or Theresa Boudreau, or call Moose Lodge on CB,* she added. *REWARD.*

"That'll find him, sure," Uncle Joe encouraged, looking over her shoulder. "We'll get the signs out as soon as we see you an' Sandy off."

"No. I...I'm going with you," Hannah said fiercely through her tears. She shot a pleading glance at Mama.

"I guess a couple more hours won't make much difference," Mama replied, her voice full of sympathy.

That morning, Hannah and Uncle Joe covered Laketon with the photocopied signs advertising for Hunter. Hannah even crammed several into the hands of southbound truckers at a truck stop.

"There's a reward, you know," she told them. Hannah had no idea how much to offer.

It just didn't seem right, asking someone to return Hunter without a reward. He was a fine dog, indeed, and she loved him. He was certainly worth everything she had to offer.

Just after noon, the boat, laden down with groceries, puttered off toward Beaver Island, with Mama at the wheel. Hannah, huddled alone on cushions in the prow, sobbed as she tried to sleep.

Chapter Nine

A Long
Long Week

Feeling lower than a dog's belly is an old saying Hannah understands. She laughed exactly once the week after Hunter disappeared.

Missy, Hunter's basset mother, waddled past as Hannah sat on the porch steps after she'd finished her school lessons. "You look like I feel," Hannah chuckled. Missy's face hung in deep doggie wrinkles, and her once sleek belly dragged the ground, her old and feeble short legs unable to lift her completely.

"Your son is lost, and you don't even care!" Hannah told Missy indignantly. Missy only rolled her languid brown eyes at Hannah and kept shuffling along.

Wednesday afternoon the CB radio crackled, and Hannah picked up the microphone. "Mama, it's Uncle Joe in Laketon," Hannah called. "He's just taken a long-distance call from Hartford, Connecticut, for us. Two duck hunters are coming tomorrow evening, and they want to know if it's okay to bring a dog or two—retrievers."

"I'm sure they can," Mama said, taking the mike from Hannah. "Harry and Walter are building a small kennel in the barn right now so we can accommodate people with dogs," Mama told Uncle Joe.

On Thursday, Uncle Joe called to say he'd heard a report from a neighbor in Laketon about a Skowhegan man who ran an illegal, unlicensed dog kennel. "The fellow sells dogs to out-of-state hunters who don't know he's not licensed," Uncle Joe's neighbor had said.

"It's a long shot, but I'm driving to Skowhegan this afternoon," Uncle Joe's voice crackled on the CB. "If that guy has Hunter, I'll report him to the Maine State Police. 10-4."

The hours seemed to creep that day, and the shadows of fall's early evening had overtaken Beaver Lodge by the time the CB radio crackled again. "This is your Uncle Joe calling from my car radio between Skowhegan and Laketon—do you read me? 10-4," came the distant, French-accented voice.

"I read you. Come in, Uncle Joe." Hannah's hands trembled, and she could barely hold the microphone.

"I found the illegal dog kennel, all right. 10-4."

"Did you find Hunter? 10-4."

"Negative. But I found a dog collar. Red. Plastic tag that says 'Hunter.' 10-4."

"Then...then he's dead," Hannah sobbed. DEAD. The unthinkable had happened.

"Not so fast, Hannah. We think he's been sold— sold to bird hunters. They were heading for the Allagash Wilderness, mebbe. 10-4."

"But how can we find him? There's several *thousand* square miles of forest between here and

Caribou!" Hannah knew her Maine geography from Mama's careful lessons in their home school.

"It's not so bad. Your puh-PAH, he has ze advantage." Uncle Joe's voice came in stronger now, as he drove north toward Moosehead Lake. "Harry—your puh-PAH—he's a licensed guide, *non?*"

"*Oui.* I mean yes," Hannah agreed.

"An' ze guides, they have ze *Bulletin* they circulate to catch night hunters, dog thieves, and ze like, do they not? 10-4."

"But that would take *weeks*, Uncle Joe." Hannah remembered that the *Bulletin*, published by the Maine Guides Association, was printed only every two weeks.

"Weeks, mebbe," Uncle Joe agreed. "But guides, they have sharp eyes for unusual dogs. I think you will get Hunter back."

"I...I wish I had as much faith as you, Uncle Joe," Hannah sobbed, hanging up the microphone.

Friday afternoon Hannah trudged to the barn to get Papa to lift a heavy chair. She silently eyed the dog cage Papa and Walt were building out of chicken wire and boards. Then Hannah quietly told Papa what Mama needed.

"Dogs!" Hannah slammed the door as she returned to the house.

"Usually you say 'rats!' when you're angry," Mama said mildly.

"I hate dogs and dog cages—anything to do with dogs!" Hannah covered her face and sobbed.

Mama sighed and busied herself with fixing supper. "We have guests coming who'll be hungry after driving all day," she said after a while to nobody in particular.

Hannah ignored Mama. She dried her tears and

dragged herself out to feed Missy, who shared Hunter's home under the porch. "There!" She realized she'd absently put enough dog food in the large bowl for two dogs, but she was not about to dump it back in the bag.

"How's it goin', sweetheart?" Papa had been especially affectionate all week, sensing Hannah's loneliness. He sat on the porch steps, waiting for Hannah to come around with the sack of dog food.

"I'm still draggin' along." Hannah forced a smile. She sat beside Papa and dropped her chin into her hands.

"You know, you're beautiful when you smile." He put his arm across her shoulders. "We're going to have to turn Beaver Lodge into a fort in a couple of years."

"Why's that?"

"To keep the boys away."

Hannah laughed. It was her second laugh in just over a week. "I miss Hunter." She turned glum again. *Do you suppose we'll ever find him?* was the question Hannah was afraid to ask.

"Sure you miss him. And I understand. I've lost folks who were dear to me, dearer than any dog. Your grandmother—my mother—for instance."

Hannah eyed Papa warily. Then she had to smile. She could always tell when Papa was working up to talk about something really important.

"Who's to blame for Hunter running off?" Papa asked gently.

"Hunter, I guess. Probably he found a stupid squirrel or a silly rabbit to follow. An' maybe it's my fault for not getting up with him when he went out the last time."

"But whom are you *really* blaming?"

"I blame God, I'm sure." Hannah was transparently honest.

"Good," said Papa.

"Good? That's bad, Papa."

"Bad to blame the Lord. Good to admit it, because you're on the way to the solution. A lot of folks refuse to admit that they blame God for what's wrong in their lives. And until they admit it, they remain miserable and frustrated. The rest of the story is, God is to blame."

Hannah's mouth dropped open. "Why that... that's..."

"God sent a gourd vine to give Jonah shade," Papa explained. "Then the Lord killed the vine with a worm so that He could teach Jonah to trust Him to care for him."

"I...I never thought about it like that before."

"Think about it. *Pray* about it. By the way," Papa added, "I phoned the *Maine Guide Bulletin* this morning. They're running a story about dog theft, and they'll include Hunter in their next issue."

"When is that?" Hannah asked.

"Two weeks." Papa tousled Hannah's hair and went indoors.

Just like Papa, Hannah thought. He always knows how to cheer me up. And Hannah did pray. She asked Jesus to forgive her anger at her loss and lift her burden. She asked Him for patience to bravely wait for the next Bulletin which was two weeks away.

Jesus answered at once. He gave Hannah peace and joy such as she'd never had, even with Hunter.

Half an hour later Hannah was taking Mama's fresh banana bread from the oven. A boat stopped at their dock, and two men in hunting clothes stepped on shore as Papa strode out to greet them.

Missy, usually quiet when guests arrived, set up such a yelping that Hannah ran to the porch to see what was wrong.

One of the men had a beautiful black and white spaniel on a leash, no doubt his retriever. "Down, Trigger," he commanded, as the dog strained and whined.

The other man had a handsome hunting hound, and it danced about in joy, if ever a dog could be joyful.

Hannah cleared the steps in a bound. The hound was Hunter!

Hannah crouched, hugging Hunter as he stood on his hind legs. He licked both her cheeks, and she kissed his nose.

Hunter's coat was sleek, and he seemed well fed. "My, you're just jumpin' with fleas," Hannah exclaimed. "I'm giving you a bath right now," she said as the guest grinned, sharing Hannah's happiness.

The man who had held Hunter by a leash chuckled. "Does everybody get this grand a welcome to Beaver Lodge?"

Chapter Ten

Table Service

"I figured the hound belonged here," explained the man who'd brought Hunter. "After I called you on the CB radio, I went into that sporting goods store in Laketon. They had a poster on the bulletin board. The thing that clinched it was the torn ear." He lifted Hunter's ear, revealing the notch where Bullet had hooked him.

"Where did you find him, Mr. Adamson?" Hannah asked.

"A gas station near Skowhegan. The man that runs the place keeps a small kennel out back. He sells dogs to sportsmen who are passing through."

"That's the place Uncle Joe told me about!" Hannah cried.

"He makes a little spare change, eh?" Papa chuckled wryly.

"I paid a hundred dollars for him," Mr. Adamson answered sheepishly. "And for a stolen dog, at that!"

"We'll pay that fellow a visit on the way home, Bob," remarked Mr. Thompson, the other duck hunter.

Papa fished two fifties out of his wallet. "I'll buy him back. You can certainly use Hunter while you're here, but you'll have to teach him to hunt," Papa chuckled. "He's never retrieved birds. Got treed by a squirrel once, though." Papa winked at Hannah.

"Well...I," Mr. Adamson stammered, taking the money. "You did advertise a reward, and your girl's got her hound back. But that guy in Skowhegan sure made a fool of me. We'll both use Trigger, here, for bird hunting." He shook his head.

※　※　※　※　※　※　※

Something was wrong with Trigger, the men's spaniel retriever. Hannah could see this at once. It wasn't even noon, yet Mr. Thompson was trudging toward the lodge, carrying his dog in his arms. A chain dangled curiously from a bulging pocket of his hunting jacket. Mr. Adamson followed closely, carrying the shotguns.

"He's hurt!" Hannah exclaimed, spotting Trigger's bloody paw. "Is his leg broken?"

"Fortunately not," Mr. Thompson growled. "But he'll be out of commission for a week, at least." Angrily he added, "Where's your father?"

"I'll get him!" Hannah ran for the shop where Papa was repairing the tractor.

"A steel beaver trap, and on my property, too!" Papa exclaimed, as soon as he reached the lodge where the hunters were nursing Trigger with Mama's help. "I assure you, gentlemen, no one has had permission to trap beaver on Juniper Bog."

"Do you own the entire bog?" Mr. Thompson asked.

"We own the entire *island* except for what's left of the old farm behind Bald Hill. That's all high ground, so no one would trap there. I'm going after those traps. Hannah, where's Hunter?"

Hannah thought she'd never heard Papa speak so gruffly.

"Please," he added, realizing that he had spoken crossly.

Hannah kept Hunter tied to the canoe as she and Papa paddled up Bog Stream. From time to time Hunter's nose would twitch, and he would whine and strain at his chain. "Another trap, Papa," Hannah would say. Sure enough, Hunter's nose, twenty-five times as sensitive as Hannah's, without fail would find the meat paste with which the unknown trapper had baited his steel traps. In several traps they found beavers struggling to get free. Papa turned them all loose, and they swam away in terror.

"I expect whoever set these traps will be poundin' on our door in a couple o' days," Papa observed when they had gathered nearly three dozen traps into the canoe.

Hannah was thoughtful as stroke after stroke, stroke after stroke, she and Papa paddled out the brook's mouth and around the island toward home in the gathering dusk.

"Can't we at least offer to let the men try Hunter as a retriever while they hunt ducks and geese?"

"We could offer," Papa said flatly. He was not convinced, Hannah could tell.

"Hunter's half Labrador *retriever*," Hannah pointed out. "It's a retriever they need, isn't it?"

"Sure is," Papa admitted. "I guess every dog's got to learn sometime."

Mr. Thompson was still sore at Papa for not telling him about the traps, even though Papa hadn't known about them either. He flatly refused Hannah's offer of Hunter's service. Even adults sometimes sulk and pout when things go wrong, Hannah silently observed.

But Mr. Adamson had grown fond of Hunter. "We'll try him first thing tomorrow. I'll do better than that. I'd like to try him in some fetching exercises this evening to see if he'll obey. Can you get me a couple of hotdogs from the kitchen?"

"Sure can!" Hannah brightened.

By starlight, Hannah watched in glee from a porch rocker as Mr. Adamson threw a stick far out into the yard. "Go get it, boy!" he'd cry. Each time Hunter returned with the stick, Mr. Adamson rewarded him with a piece of hotdog.

Then Mr. Adamson walked to the waterfront, Hunter at his heels. He threw the stick far out into the lake. "Go get it!"

Hunter did not hesitate. He plunged in and swam far out in the icy water to fetch the floating stick for his reward.

❋ ❋ ❋ ❋ ❋ ❋ ❋

"More coffee?" It was still dark as night at half past five in the morning when Hannah served breakfast to the duck hunters in the dining room as Mama worked at the stove. "Better service than at the Plaza in New York," chuckled Mr. Adamson.

"The Plaza doesn't have a buy-back program for lost dogs," growled Mr. Thompson, holding his cup out for more coffee. Since his dog had encountered the beaver trap, Hannah noticed, he had lost his enthusiasm for duck hunting. Hannah went to the kitchen where she filled a half-gallon thermos with coffee, then carefully packed corned-beef sandwiches and cookies for the men's lunch. Moments later she handed Hunter a large bowl of dog food drenched in leftover gravy from last night's supper.

"Eat up, boy," Hannah commanded. "Can't have you eating the men's ducks!"

"He won't eat our ducks. I'll see to that." Mr. Adamson came down the porch steps just then, stooping to pet Hunter. "Give him all he wants, though," he said. "A hungry dog will beg to eat our birds."

"How do you keep a dog from eating your duck when you send him to bring one in?" Hannah wondered.

"A dog can't swim and eat at the same time," Mr. Adamson laughed. "And when the dog reaches the canoe with the duck, we reward it—piece of cheese or a sugar cube, maybe."

"Are you *sure* you and your father found *all* those beaver traps?" queried a worried Mr. Thompson, coming onto the porch just then.

"Yes, sir," Hannah said. "Or else Hunter's nose is no good."

"Well, we'll take good care of Hunter," promised Mr. Adamson as he took the hound's leash.

☀ ☀ ☀ ☀ ☀ ☀ ☀

"That dog's a mongrel, Bob," Mr. Thompson reminded his friend. The men had packed for the trip home to Connecticut, and Walt was lugging their suitcases and hunting gear to the boat right after breakfast.

"He's one of a kind," Bob Adamson disagreed, with a wink at Hannah, who had just handed him a sack of doughnuts she had fried that morning for the men's trip home. "Hunter is a genuine, full-blooded Moosehead Lake retriever. Best dog north o' Boston, I'm sure!" He opened his wallet and counted out four fifties. "Two hundred dollars," he said evenly. "I'd like to own him. I'll take good care of Hunter and bring him back to see you next fall."

Hannah shot a questioning glance at Papa, who had stepped onto the porch to say good-bye to the men.

"It's your decision, sweetheart. Just don't make a choice you'll regret later," was his puzzling answer.

Big help, thought Hannah. Through her mind like a bluebird flitted thoughts of Christmas just around the corner and the nice things two hundred dollars would buy for her family at the mall in Skowhegan. Then the bluebird vanished, and Hunter came into focus, on his chain at the bottom of the porch steps. *'Regret.'* Only that word from Papa's answer stuck out in Hannah's memory. *Thanks, Papa,* she silently mouthed. "He's not for sale—not even for two thousand dollars." Hannah said out loud.

"He's a special dog, isn't he?" Mr. Adamson smiled. Then, "Excuse me. I think I may have forgotten something upstairs," he said and retreated into the house and hurried upstairs.

It was after eleven that morning, when the men had been gone several hours, that Mama asked Hannah to change the sheets in the upstairs bedroom that duck hunters had shared during their stay. "Oh! O-o-o-o-h-h!" she squealed. Pinned together under Mr. Adamson's pillow, with the same $100 Papa had paid for Hunter's return, was a brief note:

For table service better than at the Plaza, here's a little tip. Next time you go shopping, buy Hunter a sack of the best dog food in town!

Cordially,
Robert Adamson

Chapter Eleven

An
Unhappy Camper

"O-o-o-o-f-f!" Hannah struggled with a cedar rail from the pile Papa had cut the winter before.

"Heavy, huh? Let me help." Walt, who liked to show off his muscles, easily tossed the stout pole onto the trailer hitched to Papa's tractor. Today he was being nice—for a change. Now that he was spending much of his time working with Papa, Walt's attitude had improved.

"You don't have to load," Walt said for at least the fifth time. "You just came with me into the woods for the ride on the tractor. Remember?"

"I remember," Hannah sighed. "I'm going to climb Bald Hill. Holler when you're loaded to go home. C'mon, Hunter."

A fifteen-minute uphill hike brought Hannah and Hunter to an outcropping of rock on the hillside. Hannah clambered up onto it, then sat in the slanting fall sun to catch her breath. Juniper Bog was beautiful this time of year, Hannah noticed.

The low puckerbrush in the open spaces had turned crimson, and Bog Stream threaded serpentine-fashion like a thread of polished pewter, into the distant woods. Here and there stood a lonesome juniper tree, straight and tall, its needles golden in the sun.

In closer to the hill, about where the cedar grove from which Papa had cut the rails opened into bogland, a curl of smoke arose, gray and thin, into the chill fall air. Hannah slid off the rock. Whistling for Hunter to follow, she hurried back to where Walt was loading rails.

"Maybe we'd better check it out."

"Don't let it bother you." Walt was trying to be cool again, and the harder Hannah tried to get him to see that the fire could blaze up dangerously, the more he resisted.

Saying no more, Hannah walked off toward the smoke. Walt trudged after her, Hunter racing on ahead as they plunged through the cedar thicket toward the bog. Hunter's barking told them he had found something, and brother and sister began to hurry.

"Looks like we've got a squatter," Walt remarked as they came upon a small, blue pup tent hidden beneath the cedars on the bog's edge. Hunter had crowded inside, and he sniffed noisily at each item within.

"The trapper!" Hannah responded indignantly, pointing to a pile of steel beaver traps outside the tent.

"No kidding? See there!" Walt pointed to another pile, this one of flat, scaly beaver tails. "But let's check that fire out."

He strode over to where a wisp of smoke curled

up from the moss under the puckerbrush, a good ten feet from where a pile of ashes and embers showed the fire's origin. He stomped on the smoldering spot with his heavy leather shoes until the smoke ceased to rise.

※ ※ ※ ※ ※ ※ ※

"Are you sure you got it all?" Papa was not convinced when Walt assured him that he had trampled out the fire completely. "*One* ember can start burning again—you told me how far that fire traveled across the bog in the moss," Papa sternly admonished. "We'd better get the pump fire extinguishers and hurry back there. Besides, I'd like to meet that camper!

"Hannah," Papa continued, "run to the house. Tell Mama to keep her walkie-talkie on in case I need to call for help. Grab the other walkie-talkie and catch up with us in the woods. Take the shortcut across Bald Hill. Walt 'n I are going back with the tractor *on the double!*"

Hunter seemed to catch Hannah's excitement, as ten minutes later, Hannah ran up Bald Hill toward where Papa and Walt were already racing with the tractor. Though Hannah and her hound passed several rabbit trails, Hunter made no attempt to take off after a cottontail bunny or a snowshoe hare.

"Oh, my!" Hannah had reached the top, and far below, on the bogland in front of the strange pup tent, she could see Papa furiously digging a trench with a spade, while Walt, a fire extinguisher slung over his shoulder, squirted at a thin line of smoke much farther from the tent than when he and Hannah had left an hour earlier.

"Can we stop it, Papa?" Hannah cried, as soon as she reached where he was digging.

"I think so." He leaned on his shovel handle to survey the situation. "We can't let it reach the woods," he said fiercely.

Papa was mad, Hannah could tell. Mad that anyone would foolishly start a campfire in dry moss after a month without rain. He was worried, too, that the fire might spread faster than they could contain it.

"Papa—the big tractor pump!" Hannah pointed to the large pump mounted on the front of the tractor with a big reel of flat fire hose attached. Papa had used it to draw water from the lake to irrigate their gardens.

Papa pushed his hat back and frowned. "I'd get the tractor mired in this bogland muck before I got to the stream to pump water," he explained.

"I remember an old corduroy road that I crossed the night I got lost out here, Papa. It went right to the stream." Hannah pointed toward where the faint outline of an old logging road left the forest and crossed the bog toward the stream.

"Well, that should keep the tractor from getting stuck," Papa agreed. "Here!" He thrust his spade into Hannah's hands. "Keep digging a fire line!"

"Yes, sir!"

"Arf!" agreed Hunter. Hannah laughed as Hunter merrily began to dig with his paws, though he had no idea what for.

Papa soon had the tractor pump drawing water. He unwound his hose across the low puckerbrush toward the spot where Walt was trying without much luck to extinguish the smoldering fire. Even though the burning was deep in the dry moss, the mighty gush of water from the fire hose soon soaked it out.

"What's going on here?" An angry young man leaped from a canoe as soon as it hit the stream's low bank. "My traps—they're gone—every one of 'em," he said, swearing.

"Yeah. Hunter sniffed out your bait." Hannah held Hunter by the collar, for he had tried to race to meet the stranger as soon as his canoe arrived. "Without Hunter's help, we mightn't have found them all."

"R-r-r-r-r-r!" growled Hunter, baring his fangs. He seemed to sense that Hannah was angry at the stranger. Hannah was surprised. She'd never seen Hunter act so ferocious.

"Don't let that nasty mutt near me!" The strange man unsnapped his holster and rested his hand menacingly on the butt of a pistol.

"Please snap it back up, sir," Papa said firmly and evenly. "I get nervous when people do that."

The man fastened his holster and glared at Papa.

"Yeah!" Walt added. "You're gonna get arrested!"

"What for?" The man seemed surprised, as well as angry.

Papa held his hand up for Walt to keep quiet. "We saved your tent and equipment from burning up, while preventing a forest fire," he said to the man.

"*My* fire was out," the stranger protested.

"Let me show you something," Papa quietly answered, picking up his spade and striding toward the fire line, where he'd just doused the smoldering blaze with the tractor pump.

The stranger turned out to be Sam Sampson,

grandson of old Adam Sampson, who once owned the tumbledown farm back of Bald Hill. Young Mr. Sampson sobered up quite a bit when he realized he'd nearly set the woods on fire. If he had started a forest fire, he knew it might have cost him thousands of dollars in fines. Still, he snarled, "You had no right to take my traps!"

"I had no choice—and I may have saved you from being hauled into court, Mr. Sampson," Papa answered softly.

Hannah did not understand how Papa could be so kind to a man as hostile as Mr. Sampson. But then she remembered that the Bible says, "A soft answer turns away wrath," and she guessed her father knew how to use the Bible when dealing with people. After all, Hannah was aware that the Author of the Bible certainly knows human nature.

"I *do* have your traps, Sam," Papa explained. "I bought Juniper Bog from your grandfather's estate when I purchased Beaver Lodge and most of the island. My paying guests hunt ducks there. You can confirm this at the tax assessor's office in Laketon or at the register of deeds in the courthouse in Foxcroft."

"But you can't just seize my traps!"

"One of my guests' expensive hunting dogs nearly lost a leg in a beaver trap on the bog. I had no idea whose traps they were. Did I have a choice?"

"I suppose not." Sam shrugged. "But I want them back."

"Sure. Come over to the lodge anytime. Sandy'll treat you to pie and coffee," Papa chuckled.

Chapter Twelve

An Island Christmas

"That's the one—no doubt about it."

"But Walt, it's going to be too tall!" protested Hannah.

"Just right." Walt would not bend.

"Arf!" Hunter took Walt's side.

Hannah decided not to argue with Walt and Hunter.

If the balsam fir was too tall for Beaver Lodge's grand living room cathedral ceiling, Hannah knew that it could be shortened easily with Papa's bucksaw. And the extra branches could be used for decorations. Hannah had already estimated the tree's height by applying the math Mama had helped her learn that fall, but it would be unkind to Walt to argue.

"Let's cut it," Hannah cheerily agreed.

"It seems so much more like Christmas than when we lived in Skowhegan," Hannah said as she stood on the John Deere's swaying drawbar. She hung onto Walt's bouncing seat as the tree snaked and swished through the snow behind them.

Hunter, for his part, chased snowshoe hares into the underbrush, then reappeared to trot ahead of the tractor in the wheel ruts.

"Dashing through the snow,

"In a one-horse open sleigh,"

Hannah sang above the steady putt-putt-putt-putt of the tractor's two-cylinder engine.

"O'er the fields we go,

"Laughing all the way."

Walt joined her on the chorus, as together they sang:

"Jin-gle bells, jin-gle bells,

"Jingle all the way,

"Oh, what fun it is to ride

"In a one-horse open sleigh, hey!"

"The only 'bells' on this rig are those clanking tractor tire chains," chuckled Walt.

❄ ❄ ❄ ❄ ❄ ❄ ❄

"It goes clear to the ceiling," Hannah observed excitedly.

This was her family's second Christmas on the island, and like last year, they had set up a grand tree.

"I'll run upstairs for the decorations," Hannah graciously offered.

"We'll need Papa's stepladder. I'll go get it," Walt volunteered.

"No lights again this year," Walt grumbled a few minutes later, disappointed. He steadied the tall stepladder as Hannah stretched on tiptoes to place their hand-crocheted white angel at the very top.

"That's the breaks," Mama laughed, "when you don't have electricity on the island."

"It'll be my breaks if I slip," Hannah gasped. "Next year I'm goin' t' put the angel on before the tree goes up."

Hunter sat on his haunches and whined. "Silly dog," Hannah laughed at her hound.

"Can't we use candles, like they did in the old days?" Walt asked hopefully.

"No candles, except the large ones on the windowsills," said Mama. "A lot of houses used to burn down at Christmastime 'in the old days.'"

"Aw, Ma," persisted Walt, "there must be *some* way we can burn candles on the tree."

He held up a Christmas card from last year he'd found among the decorations. It was a picture, more than one hundred years old, of a group of carolers in old-fashioned clothes around a huge, candle-lit tree in a large living room.

"See here," he complained, "these folks aren't afraid of burning down their house."

"A picture is worth a thousand words," Mama chuckled, trying to be pleasant as well as philosophical. "Just the same, there'll be *no* candles on the tree," she emphasized.

Walt hunched his shoulders and slouched off. Angry, he knew that Papa would agree with Mama.

❊ ❊ ❊ ❊ ❊ ❊ ❊

The Sunday before Christmas, Walt and Hannah and their parents stayed on the mainland with Uncle Joe and Aunt Theresa after church. That evening, they would return to Laketon Community Church for the annual Christmas program.

"Let's watch TV," Uncle Joe suggested after dinner. Aunt Theresa chose *The House Without a Christmas*

Tree after Uncle Joe tossed a quarter to see who got to decide what to watch.

"Sob-story stuff," grumbled Walt as the old movie ended. "We've got the finest Christmas tree in Maine."

"Finest one on the island, at least," teased Uncle Joe.

Walt made a face at his uncle.

"I agree with you about the movie," Uncle Joe said, trying to make Walt feel better. "But someday you'll understand why women like those films," he added.

Hannah rolled her eyes and sighed. She had come to the conclusion that some movies do get a tiny corner of the Christmas story right, even if they miss the heart of Christmas. Why can't boys appreciate such things? she wondered.

※ ※ ※ ※ ※ ※ ※

As the raw wind bit her cheeks, Hannah pulled the hood of her quilted jacket tight. With her family, she roared down the lake ice toward Beaver Island late that evening. Hannah and Walt bounced in the sled behind Papa's snowmobile, and Mama sat behind Papa, clinging to his waist.

The Heart of Christmas. That had been the theme of the church's Sunday school play. *The Heart of Christmas.* Hannah ran these words through her mind again as she huddled against the wind. The story had been about a family who discovered Christmas meaning in helping others.

Afterward, the pastor had said that Jesus came, a helpless babe in a manger, not just that we might adore a baby but to show us that just as a baby is helpless, we all are helpless unless Jesus helps us. Christ came to give Himself, the pastor said.

But Christmas for me, Hannah mused, involves too much *getting*. Didn't Jesus say, "It is more blessed to give than to receive?"

"Walt is sure burning a lot of candles," Hannah worried a couple of days later. She was helping Mama clean house by scraping candle wax off windowsills with an old knife.

"Don't let it bother you," Mama said. "Walt's having fun—I guess." Mama wasn't really convinced.

"Mama, I want to do something special for Christmas this year—I want to find the real meaning of Christmas," Hannah said after a moment.

"Why not try loving someone who's hard to love? Perhaps do something for that person to really brighten his life?" Mama responded.

Hannah thought about that as she dusted the furniture and brushed up the fir needles from the Christmas tree. But there was no one on Beaver Island in real need. Even the Canadien woodchoppers had gone to Canada for a long holiday. And in Laketon? Hannah knew hardly anyone there except Aunt Theresa and Uncle Joe.

"Hannah, would you please stoke the stove with wood so the pies will finish baking." Mama held her hands up, smiling. They were covered with bread dough.

Hannah found the woodbox empty. Disgusted, she hurried into the woodshed for an armload. It was Walt's turn to fill it.

Walt? Hannah recalled Walt's hurt at having no lights on the Christmas tree. As soon as she stoked the kitchen stove, Hannah hurried upstairs to find the Christmas decorations. She found the string of a dozen colored electric bulbs she and Walt had not strung on the tree. The bulbs had no electric plug, but it would have done no good anyway, since Beaver Lodge didn't have electric outlets. Instead, two small alligator clips were attached.

Hannah hurried with the Christmas lights to the shop where Papa kept his tractor. She carefully connected the clips to the tractor's battery. The bulbs glowed at once, brilliant and beautiful!

Papa doesn't use the tractor every day, Hannah thought. I'll ask him if we can borrow its battery until after Christmas. She fondled the lights, thinking how pleased Walt would be. "Poof!" The bulbs flashed, then died.

As Hannah trudged sadly toward the house, she noticed that the plastic insulation on the Christmas lights' wires had melted.

"That's why we can't use them with the tractor battery," Mama explained as soon as she saw them. "They're six-volt bulbs. Papa's tractor has a twelve-volt battery."

"But how did people use them, then?"

"These lights were made many years ago when six-volt batteries were common, and many country folks didn't have electric lights," Mama explained. "I know you meant well," she sighed. "These old lights were left by the former owners of Beaver Lodge."

That evening, Hannah prayed that God would make this a special Christmas. "Please light Walt's life with Christmas joy," she prayed. As she blew out her kerosene lamp, she could hear Mama chatting with Aunt Theresa on the CB radio, which had its own small battery. "Yes," Mama said, "Walt's coming to Laketon on the snowmobile tomorrow morning. I need him to get a few things at the store for Christmas."

The next evening after milking Molly, Walt came into the lodge with a pail of milk in one hand and the tractor battery on a carrying strap in the other. With no explanation, he placed the battery in a box and slid it behind the tree.

"*Le* lights, they are *bonne, non?*" exclaimed Uncle Joe several days later on Christmas Eve, stomping the snow from his boots on the entry mat at Beaver Lodge.

"Beautiful!" agreed Aunt Theresa. "They are so brilliant we could see them almost as soon as we left home."

"Uncle Joe's the brilliant one," beamed Walt. "He showed me how to rewire the electric Christmas lights to use with a twelve-volt battery. I bought them at the hardware store in Laketon. The lights will make this my best Christmas ever. And Mama," Walt confessed, "I'm sorry I was rude to you about the candles."

"*Our* best Christmas ever," Hannah softly whispered.

Hunter, curled up on the braided rug beside the living room stove, opened one eye at this intrusion to his nap, then went back to sleep.

Chapter Thirteen

Hunter
to the Rescue

"Where's Walt?"

"Not back from fishing yet." Mama eyed the clock as Hannah put the last stick of wood from the box into the stove. "Four thirty. He spends far too much time on that ice now that he's built himself a fishing shanty."

"He put more work into that shanty than he would have in building Hunter a house," Hannah answered indignantly.

"Don't be too hard on Walter," Mama warned. "We've had several good meals of fried pickerel and perch from his ice fishing. *You* eat fish, too."

"I know, Mama. Want me to go get him?"

"Please do. Tell Walter to hurry. Supper'll be ready by the time you two get back. Oh, and fill the woodbox before you leave."

"Yes, Mama," Hannah glumly answered. It was Walt's turn to bring in wood. She had hoped he would get back before the stove burned out. But she was doing his chores. Again.

"C'mon, Hunter," Hannah called. Her hound was no good with firewood, but he *was* good company.

Half an hour later, Hannah and Hunter were crowded into the tiny shanty with Walt. Walt had a string of frozen fish hanging on a nail. Hunkered on an overturned plastic pail, he held a line through a hole in the ice. No sooner was Hannah inside than Walt yanked his line, then wound it onto a short, notched board. Up came a thrashing, shiny pickerel, which Hannah knew would taste good indeed with Mama's cornbread.

"Let me try it," Hannah cried.

"Okay. But hurry."

Hannah soon got a bite. She yanked, but she lost her fish.

"There's a trick to it," Walt explained. "Not like with a pole, when you can whip the pole up to set the hook."

Hannah lost another fish.

"I've got t' go," Walt grumbled. "Got t' fill the woodbox before supper."

"Walt, please. I've filled the box. And I want to catch a fish—just one!"

"Suit y'self. I'll leave the lantern to keep y' fingers from freezing."

Hannah could hear Walt's boots crunching as he marched toward home.

Ten minutes and two more lost fish later, Hannah peered outside. It was nearly dark, but a comforting glow far across the ice told her that Mama had lighted the big Aladdin kerosene lamp in the dining room.

"Ow-o-o-o-o-o-o-o-o-o," howled Hunter. *Time to go*, he seemed to say. But Hannah had to have her fish.

When Hannah finally caught one, it was a perch—and disappointingly small. "Oh, well." Hunter and girl stepped outside.

The sun had set, and light snow blew straight across the frozen lake. It was impossible to see more than an arm's length ahead even with the powerful gasoline lantern held high.

Hunter trotted off toward the lodge, and Hannah tried to follow. "Here boy! Wait!" she cried. He disappeared into the whirling snow. "If you can't see more'n I can, feller, we'll be lost 'fore we get ten feet."

"O-oo-oo-oo-oh!" Hunter protested. He was beside Hannah now, though she hadn't seen him return.

Hannah grabbed his collar. They retreated, and in half a dozen steps she bumped roughly into the fishing shanty. She clawed at the door, and when it finally opened, she hurried inside. *How long will it be before Papa comes looking? Can he even find the shanty in the dark?*

A snowmobile sputtered outside, and Hannah popped the door open. A stranger, a bearded man, crouched over the handlebars. "I'm lost," he admitted. "I'm Frank Fuller from Laketon. Been ice fishin' all day, then this snow squall comes up soon's I strike out f' home! Where are we?"

"This is Walt Parmenter's fishing shanty. We're about three hundred yards from shore. I'm Hannah Parmenter."

"We're three hundred yards from the mainland? Oh, no! You mean three hundred yards from Beaver Island."

"Yes, it's that way." Hannah pointed in the direction of Beaver Lodge, glancing hopefully at the snowmobile's headlight.

"You mean it's that way—until you take a dozen steps," Mr. Fuller muttered. "By then we'd be traveling in circles."

"Hunter will lead us," Hannah brightened. "I'm sure he can smell Mama's cooking."

"It's worth a try," Mr. Fuller agreed. "But your dog's got to have a leash. Shine your light here." As Hannah held her lantern over his vehicle, the man pulled a short piece of rope from his fishing gear. Hunter complained noisily while being hitched to the snowmobile's handlebars. "Hop on."

Hannah obeyed. Slowly they crept down the ice, following Hunter's fine nose. Then the wind shifted, and Hunter stopped, his nostrils confused by the smell of the snowmobile's exhaust fumes.

"We're lost," groaned Mr. Fuller. "Poor dog can't smell anything but the snowmobile."

"Will we freeze right here?" Hannah was frightened.

"I doubt it." Mr. Fuller's voice lacked conviction.

"Dear Jesus, help us now," Hannah prayed.

But the snow continued, cold and raw, and there were no stars out.

Yet a voice seemed to say, "Peace, be still." Hannah realized then that she was clutching Walt's heavy ice-fishing line, wound onto a board.

"Hey! I've got it!" Hannah held up the line and the lantern. "There's maybe a hundred feet here. Just let Hunter run clear t' the end of the line—he'll smell Mama's cooking instead o' the snowmobile. And we'll follow."

"Why not?" Mr. Fuller shrugged.

Hannah stood on the snowmobile's runners and played the line out to Hunter, now out of sight in the blowing snow. She felt his tug when he came to the end. "Let's go," she called to the man. "But take it slow."

After maybe ten minutes sputtering along the ice behind Hunter, Hannah's heart leaped when her line went slack. She grabbed the lantern and held it up. Above her, Hunter lay stretched out on Beaver Lodge's dock, waiting for them.

※　※　※　※　※　※　※

"Life is a lot like that lake," Papa explained as he gave Mr. Fuller a compass from the supply he kept on hand for guests. "You've got everything you need, except the most important thing. Most people don't have a clue where they're going."

"You've got that right," Mr. Fuller sadly agreed.

"Jesus is all the direction we need." Papa smiled and passed the man the compass. "Keep in mind that just as the Bible always points to Christ, this compass always points to the north—and it has a luminous dial. Point your snowmobile due southwest, and if you're lucky," Papa chuckled, "you'll see the stoplight on Main Street in Laketon before you crash into the dock."

※　※　※　※　※　※　※

"Take a look at Section B of the *Laketon Gazette.*" Walt had been to the mainland on Papa's snowmobile a week after Hunter had led Hannah and Mr. Fuller off the ice under blizzard conditions, possibly keeping them from freezing to death. Besides groceries and some things from Hanscombe's Hardware store for Papa, Walt had brought the mail and a copy of the weekly newspaper. He tossed the paper to his sister.

"Hey, hey, hey!" said Papa, looking over Hannah's shoulder.

"How did *that* get in the paper?" exclaimed Mama.

It was a large photo of Hannah and Hunter, taken on Uncle Joe and Aunt Theresa's front steps the day the Parmenter family was in Laketon for the Sunday school Christmas program. Hannah spread the paper on the kitchen table for the entire family to see.

"I told her that Aunt Theresa had pictures of me and Hunter," Hannah explained.

"Told who?" Walt insisted, curious.

"Miss Eames—the news reporter," said Hannah.

"How could that be?" Mama inquired. "You haven't been off this island in a month, except for church and Sunday school."

"A CB radio is a wonderful invention, Mama," Hannah chuckled. "I talked with the newspaper while you took lunch to Papa and Walt that day they were cutting logs in the woods."

"You didn't *call* them." Mama grew indignant. To her, it sounded a mite like her daughter had been bragging.

"Oh no, they called me!" Hannah pointed to a photo of Mr. Fuller set into the larger picture of herself and Hunter. "Ice Fisherman Finds Spiritual Message in Compass," read the caption under Mr. Fuller's picture. "Mr. Fuller was so impressed with Papa's lesson about us all needing Jesus as a compass that he went to see Miss Eames. She's the editor of the church page."

"Well, so she is!" said Papa, who now noticed "Church & Spiritul Life" across the top of the page. "Her faith in God was more important in getting off the ice in blinding snow than Hunter's nose, Hannah Joy Parmenter told the *Gazette* in an interview," Papa read aloud. "More than good luck led

Mr. Frank Fuller onto the path of a girl and her dog while he was hopelessly lost on the ice of New England's largest lake," the story continued.

Walt had said little since he'd tossed Hannah the paper.

"That's really neat," he said at last.

"Y' know, Walt," Hannah said quietly, "I didn't deserve to get my name in the paper. After all, I was foolish not to have gone home when you did."

"And if you had, Mr. Fuller might have circled in his snowmobile until he ran out of gas miles from help," Walt answered. "I guess I was a mite bull-headed to leave you out there," he sheepishly admitted.

"God uses even our mistakes to honor Him," Papa concluded. "Frank Fuller would agree, I'm sure."

Chapter Fourteen

City Cousins

"Go ahead, Uncle Joe," Hannah shouted into the CB mike. "Patch me through to Boston!"

At home in Laketon on the mainland, Uncle Joe had taken a long-distance phone call for Hannah from her cousins, the Mitchell twins of Boston, that evening early in March.

"It's ze mice," Uncle Joe chuckled. "Are you sure you want to hear zem squeak?"

"C'mon, Uncle Joe," pleaded the shrill voice on the phone, "cut the corny jokes, and let us talk to Hannah!"

"Am I talking to Miquie or Minnie?" Hannah cried, using the nicknames her cousins had chosen for themselves.

"Miquie—Minnie," both girls answered in unison. "We're on extension phones."

"What's happening in Boston?" Hannah asked. "You mice sound as excited as if you'd just won the Boston Marathon."

"We're coming to Maine—to Beaver Lodge! That is, if Auntie Sandy an' Unca Harry'll let us."

"When?" Hannah was excited now and surprised, too, because she hadn't seen the twins in two years.

"St. Pat's. We have a spring vacation from school. We plan to take the Greyhound to Laketon, if your folks can pick us up in their boat."

"I'm afraid the lake's still frozen clear across. It doesn't thaw 'til a week or two after the St. Patrick's Day holiday," Hannah explained.

"Oh-o-o-ohh."

Hannah thought she had never heard her cousins sound so disappointed. "But not to worry," she chuckled. "We can get you with our snowmobile."

"Super!" squeaked the mice.

❊ ❊ ❊ ❊ ❊ ❊ ❊

"We thought Laketon was the end of the road, but this island is really in the boondocks," giggled Miquie Mouse Mitchell, scrambling out of Uncle Joe's old four-wheel-drive pickup. Uncle Joe had driven the twins across the ice after they'd spent the night with him and Aunt Theresa.

"Yeah," agreed Minnie Mouse, close behind her sister, "you guys had such a nice house in that little village where you used to live. Why'd y' move?"

"We like it here, really," Hannah said cheerfully.

Actually, Hannah was repeating what she'd heard Mama say more than once when tourists from the city were surprised that Beaver Lodge didn't have electric lights. Hannah was certain the mice would be more polite, once they learned that her home, though it had no electric wires from the mainland, was really quite comfortable.

"Skowhegan, where we lived when you came to

visit before, is a city like Boston," Hannah corrected, certain that Minnie was merely mistaken. Skowhegan, Hannah knew, had stoplights and department stores and even a mall. "But what's 'boondocks'?" she asked, puzzled. This was a word she'd never heard before.

The mice replied only with silly snickers.

"Hannah, I need an extry pair o' eyes to turn ze truck around," said Uncle Joe, climbing into the cab.

The twins were already trudging behind Mama's toboggan, helping to push their suitcases uphill to the lodge. Uncle Joe needed someone to direct him as he backed past a big boulder at the water's edge.

"*Merci beaucoup!*" Uncle Joe thanked Hannah in French as soon as he had his old pickup pointed across the ice toward Laketon. In a quiet voice he chuckled, "Ze boondocks, it is ze end—wa-a-ay out in ze woods. Those mice, their eyes are still popping from seeing all those trees north of Skowhegan!"

"Where's the refrigerator, Auntie?" Minnie asked after lunch. The girls pitched right in to clear the table, and Minnie held the leftover soup, intending to put it away for Hannah's mother.

"We use a shelf in the pantry in the winter— saves carrying it down to the cellar," Mama said. "And always close the door, since it needs to stay cold in there."

"Then where do you get your water—from the lake?" Miquie asked, pointing to the faucets behind the sink. She had suddenly realized that since Beaver Lodge had no electricity, it probably didn't have city water, either.

Is she making fun of the way we live? Hannah asked herself, frowning. Out loud she said, "We get it from Bald Hill."

"Like 'Jack and Jill went up the hill'?" teased Miquie.

"'To fetch a pail of water,'" finished Minnie, who'd just come out of the pantry.

"No. With faucets. You can see that." Truthfully, Hannah didn't know how the water got from Bald Hill to their faucets. Until now she had not cared.

"We have a spring that fills a water tank dug into the hillside," Mama explained. "It's above the lodge, and the water comes in in a pipe."

"A spring—kind of..." sniffed Miquie.

"...old-fashioned," finished Minnie.

"There are lots of things to see and do on Beaver Island," said Hannah, trying to ignore the mice's silly remarks. "We're gonna have fun for a week!" she added pertly.

※　※　※　※　※　※　※

Hannah was surprised at how quickly the mice learned to enjoy Beaver Island's country lifestyle. "Cool," they exclaimed in unison when Mama lighted the Aladdin kerosene lamp with its brilliant mantle that glowed to fill the dining room at supper time. And they didn't complain a bit at having to use a flashlight to climb the dark hall stairs to reach their bedroom, lighted with an ordinary kerosene lamp.

"Papa says we can hitch Ebony to his pung for a drive," Hannah told the twins one day.

"Super!" they squeaked at once. "What's a pung?"

"C'mon. You'll see," Hannah laughed. "Got t' get your boots on."

In minutes, the mice had slipped into identical red boots and fur-trimmed, cranberry red parkas.

They scampered into the kitchen where Hannah, sitting beside Mama's wood-fired range, was busily lacing the high leather tops of her Bean boots.

"See y' got y' Eskimo coats on," Hannah chuckled, looking up from her lacing. "You don't need to dress so warm," she advised. "Weather's warming up."

Hannah had a nice parka, too, but she wore it only when she went to Laketon. For today she grabbed an old corduroy jacket she usually wore to the barn. She clapped a billed cap on her head, letting her French braid fall to her waist outside her coat. Too warm for my knit cap, she thought, glancing at the thermometer. But she decided it would not be nice to say any more to Miquie and Minnie about the way they were dressed.

Walt had Ebony harnessed and hitched to the pung by the time his sister and cousins reached the barn. "Hey, we saw one of those on TV—on *This New England*," exclaimed Minnie at once.

"Is it a real antique?" squeaked Miquie.

"Naw," answered Walt gruffly, "Papa made it. 'S 'most new."

Hannah decided by Walt's tough-boy answer that he had agreed to harness Ebony because he figured the girls would be gone for at least a couple of hours. Pests, she'd heard him complain one evening to Papa about the mice and their city-bred curiosity about country ways.

The pung, a heavy sled with two sets of runners, was designed for hauling logs, people, or anything that could be loaded onto it. Papa had bolted several chairs to planks so he could give his guests sleigh rides. Walt fastened two chairs in place. Before fastening a third chair, he asked Hannah, "Don't y' want a seat, sis?" he asked.

"No thanks. I'd rather stand. I can manage Ebony better with the reins that way."

"Wa-a-ait up!" Mama shouted from the porch of the lodge. "Papa forgot his lunch. He's cutting firewood over beyond Juniper Bog. Just follow the tractor tracks in the snow."

"Sure, Mama," Hannah agreed. "Hey!" she exclaimed. "Why don't the twins and I eat with him? We could have a cookout."

"Sure, why not?" Mama agreed. "But you'll need to help me pack a few more things."

When Hannah returned with a picnic basket of food, she found the mice hanging on every word as a grinning Walt explained each part of Ebony's harness. Walt even picked up a hoof like a blacksmith to show the girls how Ebony could trot on ice without slipping because of his cleated steel horseshoes. To Hannah, her brother seemed all too pleased with himself.

They're 'pests,' remembered Hannah, when they're playing with me and we're bugging Walt. How come all of a sudden the mice are such great pals to Walt when I'm not around?

Hannah did not understand herself. And she surely did not understand Walt—or her cousins.

It took about an hour to find Papa by following the old logging road across the island. Hunter alternated between riding beside the mice and darting into the woods to worry a squirrel or a hare. The twins happily pitched in, whacking dead pine branches into firewood length with Papa's axe, as Hannah laid out the sausages and rolls to brown and prepared to melt snow to make hot herbal tea. Miquie and Minnie seemed surprised that they were permitted to build a fire in the woods without a fireplace.

"With snow on the ground, there's no danger of a forest fire," chuckled Papa.

"This is really living," said Miquie, lugging an armload of dry pine to where Hannah had placed Papa's grill across two green logs.

"Yeah, like we saw them do at Plimoth Plantation," added Minnie, remembering their visit to the replica of the Pilgrim village near their home in Boston.

"Except that the Pilgrims didn't buy their sausages at the supermarket," giggled Hannah. She had never visited the Pilgrim village, but she had read about the Pilgrims.

"And they didn't use tractors and chainsaws," said Papa, nodding toward his logging equipment next to his pile of logs.

"How *did* they make sausages in those days?" the mice suddenly wondered in unison.

"Well, first you have to raise a pig," Hannah said.

"Don't go getting any ideas," warned Papa. "We have cows and chickens and a horse. That's all the animals we can manage."

"Don't forget the dog," said Minnie. "For once, Hunter didn't get any mud on my clothes."

"Arf!" agreed Hunter.

"That's 'cause he's been running in clean snow all morning, silly," Hannah snickered. These mice can be fun, after all, she thought silently.

"You girls can get home in half the time, since the bog is frozen over," Papa said when they had finished eating. He pointed out another set of tractor ruts that went straight across snow-covered Juniper Bog, rather than meander around the base of Bald Hill.

Hannah aimed Ebony down this route, and the

girls soon found themselves following a straight stretch of tracks, Hannah slapped the reins, and bracing her feet, she let Ebony trot like a sulky horse as the pung carrying three laughing cousins cut the breeze behind.

"Oh!" squealed Minnie, when they slowed down, "you look just like that sleigh driver we saw in *This New England.*"

"Sure do," laughed Miquie—"with the big boots and cap. All you need is a pipe instead of a pigtail."

"And a beard instead of freckles," Minnie giggled.

※　※　※　※　※　※　※

"You actually milk that *creature* with your bare hands?" Miquie Mitchell stood on the plank walk in the barn behind Molly one morning as Hannah pumped streams of rich jersey milk into a bucket she held with her knees. Miquie wore a Mickey Mouse sweatshirt, and her long, straight hair fell over her shoulders. Its deep red and auburn tints were highlighted by rays of the rising sun that streamed through the barn window.

Hannah watched her cousin for a moment before she replied. Both girls, she thought, had perfect hair and near-perfect faces and skin. "Sure," Hannah said, "you'd have us buy a milking machine for just one cow, maybe?"

There it was. Hannah had said it and it was too late for her to take it back.

Hannah had found her cousins' city ways irksome before their first day on the island was over. The three might have loads of fun for a few hours, but then the twins would find something about life on Beaver Island terribly funny—such as Hannah's clothes when she drove Ebony. Sometimes Miquie and Minnie could be thoughtless about not having their favorite TV shows to watch—Hannah's family had only a couple of battery-powered radios, usual- ly tuned to news or gospel programs. Or the mice would squeak when Beaver Lodge was cool in the early morning before Papa got the wood stoves burning hotly.

The early spring thaw had now made the lake unsafe to take the girls back to Laketon with the snowmobile to catch the bus, but after a week there was still too much ice to use the motorboat. Unless an Arctic chill froze the lake again, the Mitchell twins were stranded on the island until the thaw was complete. The visit that Hannah had expected to bring such joy was making everybody miserable.

"Mee-yow!" Old Tige, Papa's mouser tomcat, crept out of the shadows.

"Breakfast, Tige?" Hannah asked from her three-legged milking stool.

"Meow!" Tige agreed.

Hannah aimed Molly's teat over Tige's head and gave it a tug. Tige stretched up on his furry hind legs and caught the stream of milk without spilling a drop.

"That's fantastic," Miquie said. "Fantastic, but so-oo primitive. Gross, really."

"Tige eats *mice*. That's *really* gross," Hannah said without breaking her rhythm of pumping milk. She watched Miquie out of the corner of one eye. Since it was almost time for breakfast, Hannah half hoped to spoil Miquie's appetite.

"Mice need milk, too," Hannah laughed as she sprayed the milk again, directly onto the grinning face of Mickey Mouse on Miquie's sweatshirt.

"You...you nasty girl!" Miquie screamed. "My new shirt. I bought this at Jordan Marsh's for my trip to Maine!"

Serves Miquie right, Hannah thought, as her cousin left the barn, slamming the door. She always has to brag that she buys her clothes in the best department store in Boston. Not once did it occur to Hannah that Miquie had not even mentioned buying the shirt at Jordan Marsh until after Hannah had been mean to her.

"C'mon, Hunter," Hannah purred warmly, moments later. She set her pail of milk on the porch steps and bent to unfasten his chain. "It's warmer in the kitchen."

Hannah and Hunter found Miquie frying bacon in the kitchen of the lodge as Minnie set the table and Mama made pancakes on the other end of the old wood range. That was one thing that really burned Hannah up about the mice. They they could be finicky about feeding the chickens or milking Molly, but both twins had jumped right into the housework at Beaver Lodge since the Saturday they arrived. And Miquie had proven so good at cooking bacon on Mama's wood stove that Mama had let her take over that task.

"Here y' go, boy!" Hannah grabbed a bacon rind Miquie had left on the cutting board. Miquie had been slicing bacon directly from a slab Mama had bought in Laketon. "Treat for breakfast?" She raised her arm to toss Hunter the rind.

"Don't you *dare*. That's my breakfast!" Miquie yelled.

But Hannah had begun her toss, and Hunter snapped up his treat.

"There was bacon enough on that rind for two more!" protested Miquie.

"Mama's gone to the cellar with the milk. I'll just holler for her to bring another slab." Hannah had decided it was time to appease Miquie.

"Hunter Hound—
Mutt or clown?
Eats raw bacon
On the ground,"
Minnie teased, watching Hunter gobble up the treat.

"Mama!" Hannah called from the kitchen door to the cellar, "we're out of bacon up here!"

Mama, who had already begun to climb the steps, shot Hannah a glance that said, 'you ought to get it yourself.' Without complaining, though, she went back for more.

As soon as breakfast was over, Miquie and Minnie disappeared upstairs to the guest room they shared. Hannah figured they'd be gone an hour, at least, so she busied herself with her schoolwork while it was quiet.

That was another thing that bugged Hannah about her city cousins. They had a long session each morning showering and fixing their hair, even though they weren't going anywhere. Mama finally had to cut the mice back on their showering because it might be a couple of weeks before Papa could get to Laketon to buy more bottled gas to heat water. "They must think our hot water is on city gas, like in Boston," Mama had quietly told Papa in her only show of indignation toward her nieces.

"You could see to study better with your hair back," Mama said softly, bending over Hannah as she studied her history book. Hannah hadn't braided her hair yet that morning, and it had fallen over her eyes. So Mama quietly began to braid.

"Thanks, Mama." Whenever Mama began affectionately to fix Hannah's hair, Hannah knew that she was warming up to a loving mother-daughter chat.

"Is this island getting a mite crowded for three girls?" Mama asked.

"I'll say." Hannah thought for a moment. "Dogs and mice don't mix."

"I noticed that. The yard has turned to mud, and Hunter puts his muddy paws all over their new clothes. He doesn't understand clean, I guess," Mama sighed. "But do you suppose God let the thaw come early this spring to teach us a few things about ourselves? You don't have much contact with kids your own age, you know. Perhaps it's more than just Hunter who finds your cousins hard to take?"

"Maybe." Hannah closed her book. "This is *our* island, Mama. It's not fair!"

Mama continued to braid silently for several moments. "I don't think Minnie or Miquie wishes to be mean," Mama said at last. "But a lot of things seem unusual to them on our island. So they laugh."

"Like my clothes," Hannah snapped.

"True," Mama agreed. "But did you think they'd think *you* kind when you said they dressed like Eskimos?"

"But Mama, they wore their best coats and boots—for a ride into the woods!"

"Perhaps they wore the only outdoor clothes they brought with them. Would you take your old coat to Boston?"

"Well, I wouldn't laugh..." Hannah stopped mid-sentence as she realized that making fun of people is the same as laughing at them. " 'What would Jesus do?' That's the question they asked in *In His Steps*," Hannah said instead, remembering a book from a reading assignment.

"It surely is," Mama agreed.

"I think Jesus would try to please others," Hannah concluded.

"If that is *truly* what you have in mind, you may take today off from your studies," Mama affirmed, tying Hannah's braid with a piece of yarn.

Though Hunter whined and complained, Hannah kept him outside with Missy all day so that he couldn't bother the mice. And she kept him chained, except when she was out alone and Hunter needed to run.

Hannah set up a Monopoly board and built a cheery fire in the living room stove. She heated a pan of milk and had hot chocolate ready for the twins by the time they came downstairs.

"Miquie," Hannah said softly after they had played awhile, "I'm sorry for my rotten behavior in the barn this morning."

Miquie did not answer.

A Monopoly game can last hours, and Mama let the three girls play on. They took one break, at noon. The mice made sandwiches for the entire family, while Hannah filled the woodbox and fed Hunter. "You'll just have to be patient, boy," she told him, scratching his floppy ears. Hannah laughed as Hunter wolfed down leftover meatloaf. "I've got some cousins here, an' I think God wants me to learn to love 'em," she said.

"Ow-ooo," Hunter agreed.

"Hannah, please tote this bowl of scraps to the hens while I make supper," Mama said that afternoon, when she noticed that the girls had tired of their game. "And while you're there, see if there are any eggs."

"Sure," Hannah said. "Want t' come along?" she hollered at the twins from the kitchen.

"Nah," said Miquie, who'd begun to read a book.

"This could be interesting," remarked Minnie. "I'll go with you, long's that muddy-footed old hound is hitched." She ran for her coat.

Hannah wished at once she hadn't asked the mice to visit the henhouse. But a look from Mama said, 'Make the best of it,' and Hannah had learned from experience that God often speaks to kids through their parents.

"Gag!" squeaked Minnie as soon as the girls stepped inside the henhouse. She was wearing a new pair of expensive sneakers and had stepped right square on a fresh hen poop.

"Be glad you're not barefoot, like I go in the summer, sometimes," laughed Hannah. "There's a scraper just outside the door to clean it off," Hannah added. "That'll take care of it."

Minnie was the younger mouse by less than five minutes, so she liked to assert her independence from her older sister Miquie by doing crazy things like sewing cross-eyes on her Minnie Mouse sweatshirt. Today, Minnie demonstrated her craziness with wild ponytails, one straight out over each ear. Minnie's ponytails reminded Hannah of the feathered tail of Rusty, their Rhode Island Red rooster, but she guessed Minnie might find the comparison unkind, so she said nothing.

As the girls left the henhouse, Hannah pulled her sweater tight about her shoulders and peered westward down the lake. The clouds which had blanketed the northern wilderness with warmth for a week, were moving out, and the open sky stretched out, cold and azure, toward Canada.

"Cold front's moving in," said Papa, who had been listening to a weather report on his battery-powered radio in the barn. "You and Miquie may see Boston again after all," he teased Minnie, who was carrying the eggs. "We'll see the soft spots in the lake ice frozen hard by the end of the week, Lord willing."

The next morning Hannah asked the Lord to help her speak only kind words to the mice, even though Miquie had ignored her apology. Then she hurried to the kitchen to help Mama fix breakfast. Papa was already outside getting his John Deere tractor and chainsaw ready for his day in the woods. Walt had gone to the barn to milk Molly.

"Uh, oh!" Hannah murmured. Both pairs of her cousins' red boots were gone from the mat where they'd stood next to her Bean boots the night before. Hannah felt disgusted. She remembered how the twins had seemed so very interested in Ebony—or was it Walt—the day they had ridden over to picnic with Papa. They're probably out with Walt right now, Hannah decided. She didn't know why, but it bothered her to imagine the twins' delighted squeaks as Walt did his masculine things in the barn to impress them.

The door to the woodshed, which was attached to the kitchen, popped open. In came the mice, each piled with stovewood to their noses. Their armloads rumbled noisily into the woodbox beside the wood-fired range.

"Hi, Hannah!" chirped Minnie.

"We're takin' your turn fillin' the woodbox,"

squeaked Miquie, nodding toward the small black-board where Mama kept a record of chores.

"Yeah, an'..." said Minnie.

"...we're sorry we've been kinda mean," apologized Miquie. "And we forgive you, too," she added.

Hannah smiled, grateful for the truce, and the three cousins hugged. Then the mice scurried back to the woodshed for another armload of wood.

❊ ❊ ❊ ❊ ❊ ❊ ❊

"We had a great time, Hannah," Miquie cried as the bus driver stashed the twins' luggage underneath the Greyhound. "And I even fed Hunter this morning," Miquie added, patting Hunter, whom Hannah held on his leash.

"She kissed his nose, too," Minnie giggled.

"Well, he *hadn't* been eating mice, like that disgusting barn cat," the other mouse mocked, faking indignation.

The girls all laughed, glad they could now joke about their misunderstandings.

"Come visit us in Boston," Miquie urged, giving Hannah a quick hug and a kiss on the cheek. Then Minnie, crazy ponytails intact, kissed her cousin, too.

Moments later, as the big bus pulled out of Laketon's station, Hannah found herself crying. Only days earlier, she knew, she most likely would have stayed at Beaver Lodge while Mama took the mice on the snowmobile to Laketon.

Chapter Fifteen

Tears for Two

"This one, Auntie," Hannah squealed in delight. Hannah held up the wool skirt for her aunt's inspection. It was a genuine Black Watch plaid.

"Handwoven in the Outer Hebrides of Scotland," Aunt Theresa read aloud from the fabric tag. "Nice material," she said. Aunt Theresa showed Hannah the price tag. "$90" had been crossed out and "$50" written in, then "$30."

"Closeout sale, ma'am," explained the clerk at Stern's Department Store, in Skowhegan mall.

"C'n I try it on, Auntie?" Hannah asked.

"Sure. At that price I'll pay for it myself."

"What do you think?" Hannah asked moments later.

"It fits you beautifully," Aunt Theresa agreed. "There's a problem, though."

"What's that?" Hannah frowned.

"You're a growing girl."

"'Almost a woman.'" Hannah liked to recall what Papa said.

"Indeed! By fall that skirt will be too small."

Hannah wanted to protest that she could still wear the skirt for two or three more Sundays in this northern climate. But since it was Aunt Theresa's money, she was politely silent.

"Do you have this in a larger size?" Aunt Theresa asked the clerk.

"I'll check the stockroom."

Hannah's hopes rose as moments later the smiling clerk returned with a larger size folded across one arm.

The two-week visit with Aunt Theresa and Uncle Joe during Moosehead Lake's ice-out would bring Hannah and Walt home just a week before Easter. While staying with their aunt and uncle, they spent part of each day at Laketon Christian Academy. Here, the teachers helped them catch up on schoolwork by filling gaps in home-schooling lessons that Mama had not been able to help them with. Besides taking quarterly tests, they had lab experiments for science classes and computer work to do.

When the lake was completely thawed, their parents would come to get them in the motorboat. Today however, Hannah and Walt were shopping in Skowhegan with Uncle Joe and Aunt Theresa.

※ ※ ※ ※ ※ ※ ※

Palm Sunday came bright and beautiful in Laketon on Moosehead. Hannah was surprised that she had slept until the sun rose, for on Beaver Island she was up before dawn. "Oh, well," she yawned.

"O-o-o, o-o-o, o-o-o!" Hunter whined, scratching at the bedroom door.

"Got t' go out, boy? Well, c'mon." Hannah grabbed her corduroy bathrobe, then slipped her feet into her slippers. Snapping her hound's leash onto his collar, she hurried downstairs.

The frosty air stung Hannah's cheeks as she stepped outside with Hunter, and ice from small puddles left by yesterday's brief rain tinkled beneath her buckskin slippers. What a beautiful day to try out my new skirt, she mused. Hannah frowned, remembering that Aunt Theresa had bought it two sizes too large, for wear next fall.

"If your mother wants to pin it up so you can wear it for Easter next Sunday, I guess it would be okay," she had said. "But unless your mother says it's all right, I insist you put it away until you grow some more."

Aunt Theresa, who had no children, was not like Mama, Hannah considered. Though Mama would have pointed out that it wouldn't fit right, Hannah would have been allowed to decide for herself.

Even though Aunt Theresa didn't understand that kids like to make their own decisions, she did know that kids like to eat. Breakfast was home-made waffles soaked in frozen raspberries and topped with real whipped cream. Aunt Theresa's large berry patch and garden always gave her plenty for the freezer, and there was nothing Hannah liked more about spending a couple of weeks with Uncle Joe and Aunt Theresa than the meals from that freezer.

After breakfast, Hannah joined Uncle Joe and Walt who were watching a church service on the living room TV. The choir of several hundred voices was marvelous. Hannah found it hard to imagine even a church as large as that choir.

When the TV pastor preached about children obeying their parents, Hannah's ears burned. Hannah had chafed for these two weeks because Aunt Theresa and Uncle Joe had different standards from her parents. It had been hard to obey Uncle Joe and Aunt Theresa, even though both Mama and Papa had instructed her and Walt to do so. How good it would seem to get back to the island where she didn't need to blow-dry and curl her hair every morning or wear a prissy dress to school.

Speaking of dresses. Hannah shot a glance at the clock. Nearly nine—time to dress.

"The car leaves at 9:15," Uncle Joe warned as Hannah dived for the hall door and bounded up the stairs.

The new wool skirt was on its hanger on the closet doorknob. Hannah made a quick decision. Mama had sent along a handful of safety pins for emergencies. Why not at least see what it looked like with her new sweater? More than once, Hannah remembered, Aunt Theresa had made a 'final' decision, then changed her mind. Besides, she reasoned, even Aunt Theresa would admit she sometimes doesn't understand girls.

Hannah folded the skirt up, pinning the heavy material in place. Then she slipped it on, took a tuck in each side, and pulled the zipper up. She twirled before the full-length mirror like a cheerleader. "Super! What d' y' think, feller?"

"O-o-o-oh," Hunter rolled his languid brown eyes warily.

"At least you could say it's nice."

"Arf!" Hunter agreed.

"That's better." She pulled her new white velour turtleneck over her head, smoothing the tail over the skirt's waist to cover the tucks.

"Swell!" That was an old-fashioned word Mama used, and Hannah tried it out when she especially wanted to feel grown-up.

"Oh, my!" Hannah exclaimed, seeing that Uncle Joe was sitting in his car with the motor running. Walt was already in the back seat, and Aunt Theresa was just going down the front steps. Hannah grabbed her coat and Bible and raced downstairs.

☀ ☀ ☀ ☀ ☀ ☀ ☀

"There certainly *was* a *wet paint* sign on that banister!" Miss Helen Crosby shook her head in dismay as she examined the white stains on the black and forest green of Hannah's new wool skirt. "The men had a work bee yesterday to get ready for Easter, but it was cool last night, so the paint hadn't dried," explained Miss Crosby, Hannah's Sunday school teacher. "There may be a can of paint thinner in the supply room that we can try."

There was little conversation in the car as Uncle Joe drove Aunt Theresa, Walt, and Hannah to the Boudreau home after church. The April weather had turned warm, and Hannah found that heavy wool itches like crazy when one begins to sweat, even through a cotton slip.

"I'm cold," Walt growled, almost as soon as Hannah lowered a rear window to get some fresh air. She rolled the car window back up, deciding it was best to add discomfort to her misery of conscience, after all.

Angry at her own foolishness in damaging her new skirt, a not quite penitent Hannah raced into the house and flew up the stairs as soon as Uncle

Joe braked to a stop in the drive. She ignored Hunter, chained to the porch swing and begging to be set free, and ran straight to her room. Hannah had not yet packed the paisley cotton jumper she'd planned to wear to church—in fact, it was still spread out on the bed. Hannah fairly leaped into the jumper. Then, her nostrils offended by the odor of paint thinner, she hung her wool skirt across the back of a chair, pushed the chair next to a window, and pulled the window open.

"I should have let you decide for yourself," Aunt Theresa fussed Sunday afternoon. Miss Crosby's powerful paint thinner had taken the paint off, but it had also removed some of the dye from the wool, leaving the material with faded spots. Hannah might still wear the skirt, but not for her best.

Hannah looked at her aunt, puzzled. "Why should you have let me decide?"

"Because then you wouldn't have added disobedience to carelessness," Auntie said, hurt that Hannah had ignored her instructions.

I didn't really plan to disobey, Hannah thought. But her conscience told her that she hadn't really *planned* to obey, either.

A spring thundershower after midnight took the last of the ice from the lake. Hannah propped herself up on pillows and watched the stormy lake lit up by brilliant bolts of lightning. Once or twice the electrical display lighted distant Beaver Island, pulling from Hannah's soul every feeling of homesickness a girl could have. Tomorrow was Monday, and Mama and Papa would come for her and Walt, but Hannah wanted to go home now.

The storm let up at last, and Hunter whined to go out. Hannah slipped down the back stairs with her dog and led him out the back porch door. After Hunter returned, Hannah crept into the kitchen for a drink.

Hunter padding behind her, Hannah crossed the living room to reach the front stairs. Then she froze. Curled in her robe in an armchair, Aunt Theresa sat sobbing. "O-o-ow," worried Hunter. Auntie looked up.

"Upstairs, boy," Hannah commanded. She slipped to Auntie's chair and sat on the arm. For a moment Hannah became the woman and her aunt the girl as Hannah kissed the dear, salty cheek of Mama's older sister. Hannah's grandmothers had both died before she was born, but Hannah had developed such a bond of affection for her Aunt Theresa that she was like a grandma to her.

"We're going to miss you kids, Uncle Joe and I," Auntie said. Her voice was weepy and broken.

"I'll miss you, too," Hannah admitted. After a long silence, Hannah added, "Do you miss not having children?"

"More than you can imagine, darling." Aunt Theresa pulled Hannah close.

"Auntie," Hannah murmured at last, "I love you. And I'm sorry I disobeyed."

"The skirt," Auntie said, drying her tears on her robe, "is not important. Love is important."

Hannah finally fell asleep that night remembering the words of Jesus: "If you love me, keep my commandments."

Hannah wore her wool skirt for two winters, and fortunately the faded spots became less noticeable each time Hannah washed the skirt by hand. Never would Hannah let Mama put it in the washing machine, nor would she ever let Mama wash it herself by hand.

Something about a lesson in love, obedience, and responsibility came back to Hannah each time she wore her tartan skirt. Though the details of the paint spot accident grew dimmer and dimmer in Hannah's memory as the months marched onward, the lesson of the skirt remained bright and new.

Chapter Sixteen

A Poke
in the Nose

"Where y' headed, Walt?" Walt left the John Deere idling at the kitchen door as he hurried inside.

"Papa's logging camp. Doughnuts ready?"

"Sure," Hannah brightened. "Want some t' go?"

Walt crammed a doughnut between his teeth without answering. "Hey," he mumbled, "good as Mama's."

"Of course! Mama taught me how. What're you going over to the cabin for?"

"Papa and I need that steel crowbar he let the loggers use. We're building fences. Want t' come along?"

"Yeah, I'll get my jacket."

"C'mon, Hunter," Hannah called moments later, whistling. Her hound shot out from beneath the porch and ran straight through a mud puddle. Hunter reared on his hind legs and plopped both muddy paws on Hannah's clean jacket. "Mud doesn't mean a thing to you, does it, feller?" she laughed.

"Since Papa said I can let you run, you're into everything!" Hannah gently set Hunter on all fours, then scraped the mud from her coat.

Hannah hopped onto the tractor's drawbar, then clung to the seat behind Walt, who drove. Hunter trotted behind or raced ahead, wherever his sharp nose led him.

Their first stop was the barnyard gate. Hannah, in her old Bean boots, hopped off into the mud to let the bars down so that Walt could drive the tractor through. More bars appeared at the far side of the barnyard. Without complaint, Hannah wrestled these open, then dragged them shut after Walt drove the tractor through.

They crossed the pasture to the edge of the woods. Walt pulled up to the bars and sat idly, resting his arm on the steering wheel.

Hannah waited.

"Ain't y' goin' t' open the bars?"

"Your turn, big brother." *I'm not your slave* flitted wickedly through Hannah's mind, but she bit her tongue.

Walt did not answer as he hopped across the big tractor wheel into the muddy road and grudgingly yanked the bars open.

Hannah climbed into the tractor seat at once. She opened the gas and pushed the hand clutch, like she'd done when Papa had her drive in the field as he and Walt loaded hay.

"What do you think you're doing?"

Hannah stopped the tractor as soon as it entered the forest, then climbed down. "Just thought I'd be helpful, long's I'm here," she teased.

"Okay," Walt grumbled.

A Maine forest is an empty place in April,

Hannah thought. She found that she could see all the way from Bald Hill, clear out onto Juniper Bog, where the silver thread of Bog Stream swam serpentine beneath a springtime sky.

Hunter was not seen for some time, but Hannah was unconcerned. The times he had gotten loose from his chain, he'd always come home. And since he couldn't get off the island, Hannah knew she wouldn't lose him again.

The shrill call of a bluejay rang through the leafless forest, the bird flitting from treetop to treetop, warning the world of the woodland that Hunter the terrible Hound, ferocious enemy of all who wore fur or feathers.

"That jay thinks he's in charge of the woods," laughed Walt as they puttered along.

"Hunter couldn't catch a drowned rat," Hannah chuckled.

The cabin soon appeared around a bend in a clearing where the Canadiens had cut logs for the paper mill. Ricks of logs were stacked next to the tractor road.

Here was Hunter, his hindquarters sticking out from beneath the cabin, his tail going around like a fan.

"Come out of there!" Hannah cried. "If it's a skunk we don't want it."

Hunter backed out and trotted obediently to his mistress. Hannah petted him. "Why, you're all trembling," she murmured. "You must have seen an animal in there."

"Hannah!" Walt yelled. "Come in here!"

"C'mon, Hunter!" Hannah raced inside.

"What do you make of this?" Walter held a broom in one hand and an axe in the other. The wooden handles of both implements had been gnawed down to stubs.

Walt held them up to the light. Tiny tooth marks were all over the stubby pieces of handles.

"A squirrel, maybe?" Walt asked. "No beaver could get in here. Hole's too small." He pointed to a small hole in the floor, where tooth marks, like those on the handles, appeared. Hunter's nose was in the hole in an instant, and he scratched furiously at the floor, trying to make it larger so he could get through.

Hannah laughed. She laughed and she laughed and she laughed until the tears ran. It was unusual for Walt to ask her opinion about anything.

"What's so funny?"

"Porcupine. A porcupine has a winter den right under this cabin. That's what Hunter's after." Hannah quickly shut the door.

"But why would a porcupine eat wood?" said Walt. "Wood isn't food."

"Porcupines love salt. I learned that in a report I wrote on animals of the northern forest."

"Salt? Oh! You mean, people use the broom and the axe with bare hands. They sweat. Porcupines eat them for the salt."

"You got it," Hannah agreed.

Hunter was scratching at the door.

"Hunter!"

Hunter got his nose through. The door flew open, and he was gone!

Hannah raced outside. "Hunter! Come back here! Now!" she screamed.

Hunter kept on running. He tore off after a small gray animal that waddled as it went.

"That animal must be sick," said Walt, who'd

just come outside. "It's not even trying to get away. Why doesn't it climb a tree?"

"Hunter!" shouted Hannah.

Just then Hunter pounced on the creature, snapping at its neck.

"Yipe! Ow! Ow! Ow!" It was not Hunter's victim crying in pain. It was Hunter, the disobedient hound. Hunter raced back like a shot. "Ooo-ooo, ooo-ooo, ooo-ooo." Hannah thought she had never heard such pitiful cries. She carefully held Hunter's collar.

"Porcupine?" said Walt, amazed. "I'd rather tackle an alligator."

"Give me a hand!" Hannah gasped.

Walter, who wore leather gloves, picked out the poisonous porcupine quills stuck inside Hunter's delicate mouth. But as soon as the quills were gone from his mouth and he could close it once more, Hunter began to snap and snarl viciously, making it impossible for Walt to remove the quills from Hunter's tender nose.

"What'll we do, Walt?" Hunter's eyes had begun to swell shut, and he surely could not see to trot home.

"Let him ride on the tractor with us, I guess," said Walt. "That is, if we can get him up there without getting stabbed."

"We're *not* leaving *my* Hunter," Hannah answered determinedly.

Walt had little pity for Hunter, who in his opinion had merely been stupid. But like Hannah, he realized that Hunter could not simply be left behind. So Walt strode toward the cabin, as Hannah held Hunter. "I dunno what I'm goin' in here for," he said, disgusted at the inconvenience

Hunter had caused. "Still maybe there's something in there we can use."

Soon, Walt came out carrying a ratty old quilt. "Found this under a bunk," he growled, holding it up for Hannah's inspection. "Now if we can just wrap your dog in it so he can't fight."

"Good idea," Hannah agreed.

Walt spread the blanket on the ground behind the tractor.

Hannah lay Hunter on it, folding his legs gently. Hunter did not resist. Blinded and in pain, he seemed to feel the need of her loving attention.

"Guess I won't need this," Walter grumbled, removing his belt. "I'll be drivin' the tractor."

He wound the leather belt around the hound, making a neat bundle. Careful not to bump Hunter's quill-bristly nose, Walt boosted the dog onto the tractor. "Be a sight if I got bit loadin' this dog," he remarked.

They puttered toward home on the John Deere, Hannah standing on the drawbar and steadying Hunter as best she could. Half an hour's slow progress brought them to the stretch of corduroy road about a mile from home.

"Walt!" Hannah screamed suddenly as the tractor's wheels rumbled onto the rough logs of the corduroy, "Slow down!" The bouncing had caused Hunter to bump his nose, and he had begun to fight to get out of the blanket.

"Ouch! Stop, Walt, please!"

Walt stopped the tractor. "What's going on?"

"I just got poked with a quill right through my leather gloves. I've got to walk and carry Hunter."

"Suit y'self."

Hannah hopped off, then cradled Hunter in her arms.

Walt drove off without looking back.

Hannah was not lonely, but she *was* angry. She was angry with Walt. After all, he could have taken a turn at carrying the wounded hound while she drove the tractor

"And I'm mad at you for tackling that dumb porcupine," she told Hunter, while resting on a rock just before they left the forest into the open pastureland. Then Hannah laughed. She laughed at the silliness of God's using a dog to teach a girl things about herself.

Hannah laughed again. "It's not God who's silly," she concluded. "It's silly me. I guess I don't learn obedience so well, either," she said, remembering the plaid wool skirt.

Hunter's nose had swollen to the size of an orange by the time the two reached Beaver Lodge. But with Papa's help, Hannah managed to remove the rest of the barbed quills with a pair of needle-nose pliers.

Porcupine quills are poisonous, and though Hannah and Papa got them all out, Hunter's doggie face remained puffed up for several days. Though it was cool weather, Hunter trotted around with his crooked mouth open, his tender tongue hanging out, and one eye swelled shut.

"Hard lesson, huh, boy." Seated on a low stool, Hannah lovingly cradled Hunter's head on her knees as she fed her hound the way a hospital nurse feeds a patient. Since Hunter's condition made it impossible for him to eat hard, dry dog food, Hannah had mixed him a tasty paste of boiled cornmeal mush and bacon drippings. Hunter's appetite was still strong, but Hannah winced as he took each painful bite.

"Some of us have to learn our lessons the hard way, I guess," Hannah murmured to Hunter one day. She was nursing him back to health, and his sorrows were her sorrows, his hurts, her hurts. "I guess it's not just houn' dogs that have t' learn by experience," Hannah added softly.

It was only a few short weeks later when, "Hunter!" Hannah shouted from the porch of Beaver Lodge one morning in May. A skunk had burrowed beneath Mama's henhouse, and Hunter was trying to dig the egg thief out. But he came running at once when Hannah called.

"You want to catch that nasty ol' skunk, don't y' boy? Let's let Papa catch it with a trap, instead."

"Rufff!" Hunter happily agreed, rubbing his silky coat against his mistress's legs. He had learned obedience at last.

Chapter Seventeen

A Hound Hospital

"What's Walter doing with the tractor all morning?" Hannah was helping Mama hang wallpaper in an upstairs bedroom to get ready for the tourist season. "He's driven from the barn to the dock with the John Deere and trailer at least a dozen times."

"You know Papa has canoes and pontoons stored in the barn that he needs to get to the waterfront," Mama explained.

Hunter, for his part, had spent most of the morning seeking the best places to sleep. The earth was still too cool for comfort in late May, but the sun shined too hot for comfort without shade, so his options for doggie comfort were limited indeed.

The "pop-pop-putt-pop" of the idling tractor motor had made Hannah nervous, so that she hung a sheet of wallpaper crooked. "What a mess!" she snapped. "*Why* has Walt left that noisy tractor running in front of the house?"

"I'm sure he's only using the bathroom," said Mama. "Now let me help you before that gets torn."

"YIPE!" Hannah had not heard Hunter cry so pathetically, not even when he'd tackled the porcupine. She hopped off the step-stool, where she'd just corrected the crooked wallpaper, and raced to the window. Walt had stopped the tractor, and he ran to where it had just been parked by the porch steps.

And there lay Hunter's poor body. He had obviously taken a snooze on the warm gravel drive in the trailer's shade while Walt was in the lodge. The trailer's dual wheels had gone right over him.

Hannah *had* to be dreaming. She loved Hunter, and he could not be dead! She stared, gripping the windowsill. Then Hunter's tail twitched, and Hannah's trance broke. She ran downstairs two steps at a time.

No mother had ever held an infant more lovingly than Hannah held Hunter. "I love you, baby. Please don't leave me," she cried.

But the soft spots where Hunter was supposed to have ribs and the blood oozing from his nose told her that only the merest thread held Hunter's life in the land of the living. One hind leg hung limply, and his furry skin was peeled off most of one bleeding hip.

"It will cost $250, maybe $300 to patch him up—*at least*. I'm sure he'll respond to home nursing as well."

Papa's voice came through the open door as Hannah, in the kitchen, heated water on the gas stove for a hot water bottle.

"I just talked with the vet on the CB," Papa added to Walt. "We can't afford it. We're barely paying our bills as it is."

"What did people do for hurt pets before there

were vets?" Hannah sobbed to Mama. Hannah knew Papa was right, though she could hear the sympathy in his voice.

"Put them to sleep." Mama patted Hannah's head.

"I can take care of him, if he's not going to live anyway," Hannah heard Walt whisper to Papa. "I'll bury him, so Hannah doesn't have to watch." Walt sounded upset and worried, Hannah thought.

"You've said enough—too much," Papa quickly warned just before they stepped inside.

"I'm staying with Hunter no matter what happens," Hannah said fiercely. "Thanks anyway, Walt."

Walt didn't understand Hannah's grief, and she didn't understand his feelings. But this was no time for anger, Hannah decided.

Mama gently held Hannah. "Walt has some things to learn," she said.

"Walt, I'm sending you to the vet in Laketon with the motorboat," Papa remarked, as soon as he had checked Hunter over. "We'll need a syringe of antibiotics to stave off infection. Better get a syringe of painkiller, too. I think I can set his bones with wooden splints, but it's best if he's out when we do so. While you're gone, Hannah and I will work on the bleeding."

"Your hound's seen more grief in a little more'n a year on this earth than any two town dogs would see in a lifetime," Papa said in amazement, as he and Hannah worked to stop Hunter's bleeding. "When we lived in Skowhegan, several of our neighbors had dogs, but I don't once recall one of them getting hurt. We lived on a busy street, too."

"They say cats have nine lives," Hannah

answered grimly. "Hunter's been tossed by a bull, stolen, poisoned by a porcupine. That's three. Now he's been run over."

"Five to go," said Papa. "Hannah, I don't wish to be discouraging," he added, "but Hunter's chances of surviving this one are very slim, indeed. If he doesn't bleed to death internally, he may die later of infection."

"I know, Papa. But why are you telling me this?" Hannah began to cry silently.

"You need to be prepared. It's only realistic."

"That doesn't *sound* like you at all," Hannah said, wiping her tears on her sleeve. "Just the other day you were talking to me about faith."

"That I was." Hannah had Papa stumped for a moment. "Remember though," he said after several thoughtful moments, "faith isn't just believing that something will happen, then expecting it to come to pass. That's wishful thinking."

"Like wishing on a star," said Hannah.

"Exactly."

It was Hannah's turn to be thoughtful. "I guess faith is trusting God, no matter what."

"I'd say that's a pretty good definition," Papa agreed.

"So, no matter what happens to Hunter, I will still trust God to do what's best by me."

"You got it, Honey."

"Know what, Papa? If Hunter pulls through this—or if he doesn't—I can say I've been happy with him for a time, can't I?"

"IKE!" Before Papa could answer, Hunter's complaint brought father and daughter back to the task at hand.

Hunter did heal, but slowly, over the next two

months. He became a baby again, sleeping long hours in a box of rags in the kitchen or on the porch on sunny days. Hannah fed him milk and medicine from a baby's bottle. During the early weeks of summer, she watched his eyes grow bright and his muscles grow strong enough so that he could stand up on shaky legs.

During the weeks that Hunter was healing, Hannah wrestled with anger. Walt had run over her dog, then volunteered to put him out. Was he really being unfeeling? she asked herself. Could she really, truly forgive her brother? Had he even wronged her? she pondered.

Chapter Eighteen

Hannah Gives Hunter Away

"Travis had to shoot Old Yeller, Mama."

Hannah had been fighting tears all morning. A good book can sometimes worm its way into a girl's heart as if it were truly alive.

Hannah cracked another egg onto the gas griddle, making breakfast for the family of tourists waiting in the dining room. "Mama, *please* watch the eggs." Hannah grabbed a dish towel and rushed to the porch steps.

In a moment, Hannah was back, her tears dried. Mama was busy serving eggs and bacon and refilling coffee cups by then, so Hannah hurriedly flipped the pancakes to keep them from burning. Mama was usually the cook and Hannah the waitress, but when there were guests to serve, mother and daughter covered each other's job whenever necessary.

To tell the truth, Hannah felt a mite guilty for leaving Mama right in the middle of breakfast. But when one has to bawl, one has to bawl, she decided.

"Coffee?" Hannah asked the vacationers moments later. She had taken a fresh pot made on the wood stove to the dining room. Mama liked to fire up that stove alongside the gas during these cool Maine summer mornings. A little warmth in the kitchen felt good, and stovewood was plentiful, while bottled propane gas had to be toted in the boat from the mainland. Coffee pot in hand, Hannah now waited for the guests' reply.

"Please!" It was Mr. Achterhoff, whom Papa said was a judge from Connecticut. Directly from the hot pot, Hannah poured a flawless stream into Judge Achterhoff's cup—and she ran it over.

"Oh, my! I'm sorry!"

The judge frowned. Mrs. Achterhoff forced a smile.

In her imagination, Hannah had been in the dry-grass country of West Texas more than a hundred years ago, fighting bears, wild boars, and rabid wolves. She rode a mule named Jumper, and a big yellow dog raced alongside them. Hannah's hand had stretched down those hundred years, across more than a thousand miles from Texas to Maine, to pour coffee. And her hand had poured and poured and poured as Old Yeller—or was it Hunter?—was torn by the sharp tusks of mean old boars. Embarrassed, Hannah apologized again and made a quick exit as Mr. Achterhoff sopped up the spilled coffee with his napkin.

"You were surely way out in Texas when you spilled the coffee," Mama chuckled half an hour later, after the Achterhoffs had paddled off in a canoe. "You were pretending to be Travis."

"Not pretending, Mama," Hannah said earnestly. "I *was* Travis." Hannah's ears burned red when she realized what she'd said. "I mean, I can't be Travis, can I? Travis is a guy and I'm a girl. But there are many things guys and girls have in common—like loving dogs, for instance."

"You were really Hannah, and you still are," Mama said with a smile. "But you're right. If a book cannot become a part of the reader, it is a very poor book, indeed."

"This morning I was really in Texas," Hannah affirmed, happy that Mama understood. "The Civil War had just ended, and I was alone with *you*. With you and my little brother Arliss and an old yellow stray dog called Yeller, whom I loved."

"Like you love Hunter," Mama laughed.

"And you know what, Mama?"

"What?" Mama wiped her hands on her apron and hugged Hannah close.

"Each time I read the part about Travis having to shoot Old Yeller when he got rabies, I bawl like I'd just shot Hunter. I know it's fiction, but it was so real that I *was* Travis. Is that wrong, Mama?"

"I think," Mama said, "that God sometimes lets us respond emotionally—by crying or laughing at make-believe stories, for instance—to help us learn real things about ourselves and others."

❄ ❄ ❄ ❄ ❄ ❄ ❄

Hannah awoke just after midnight to the rumble of doggie feet on the third-floor stairs above her bed. Walt slept in the attic at Beaver Lodge during the summer, since his second-floor bedroom was needed for paying guests' use. But why was Hunter trotting up there?

As usual in warm weather, Hannah had left

Hunter chained by his home beneath the porch. Hannah's hound got to sleep on her bed only in freezing weather, after he'd been thoroughly treated for fleas. Hannah was too sleepy to stay awake wondering about it for long, though.

There it was again! A gunshot. Startled awake, Hannah held her ticking brass alarm clock up to catch the moonlight. 3:15. She hugged her bed and strained to listen. Another shot was followed by the booming bay of Hunter's grand voice in the quiet night.

Hannah slipped to a chair by the window over the porch. Two figures with shotguns, one with a flashlight, the other with what looked like Papa's gasoline lantern, raced across the cornfield next to the barn.

Soon the men strode toward the house, Hunter at their heels. One was Papa who hurried directly up the steps. The other, Walt, stopped to hitch Hunter to his chain.

Hunter whined and complained.

Walt stooped and scratched Hunter's floppy ears. "Good boy," Hannah heard through the screened window as Walt whispered so as not to disturb the sleeping guests, "You've been a fine coon hunter tonight. I guess you've earned the right to sleep inside. C'mon."

Walt unsnapped Hunter's chain, and soon Hannah heard boy and dog sneaking up to the attic.

Hannah struggled with her feelings until daybreak. Fully awake, Hannah, who hours earlier had put herself and Hunter into the book instead of Travis and Old Yeller, now imagined Walt replacing Travis as Hunter's companion. Maybe Hunter would make her brother as happy as he made her and as Old Yeller made Travis. I'd do almost anything to make him happier, she sighed. Hannah loved brother Walt, and his surly attitude made her heart ache.

Sometimes Hannah wondered if Walt loved Jesus the way she did. She knew that made a person happy. But, Hannah knew she shouldn't judge. Besides, she considered, Walt always has his Bible lesson done for Sunday school, and he's won several awards for Bible memorization. Maybe Walt just needs a friend, someone to love, she mused. Perhaps I've been selfish with Hunter.

Hannah recalled the many times when, chained to the porch, Hunter patiently slept in the sun while she helped Mama in the house. Sometimes Walt would take Hunter along when he worked with Papa in the fields or woods. But mostly, Hunter waited for Hannah, and he would trot by her side when she fed the chickens or race to the waterfront when Hannah needed to help a guest launch a canoe from the boathouse. Perhaps Hunter and Walt belonged together.

The early rays of dawn had just begun to light en the top of Mt. Kineo when Hannah pulled a sheet of paper from a box of her best stationery. She laid it on the windowsill and began to write:

Brother Walt,

I'm giving you Hunter as a love gift to keep.

Does that sound corny? Hannah thought. No, that's what I want to say. I do love Walt.

Hunter is yours from now on. A dog is a boy's...

Hannah stopped writing. She erased 'boy's,' then continued:

...man's animal. He needs to be following YOU around the island, instead of staying tied up all day.

> *Love,*
> *Hannah*

After sneaking up the attic stairs, Hannah slipped the note under her brother's door. She then crept back to her room, where she crawled beneath her blanket and sobbed until Mama called her to help with breakfast.

Chapter Nineteen

A Dog Who Likes No Other

"Night hunting is making a baa-ad doggie out of you."

Hannah stopped to pet Hunter on her way to the house from gathering eggs. He was asleep on his chain at the end of the porch, and he merely opened one tired eye and whined as she bent to scratch an ear.

"Why, you're just hoppin' with bitin' fleas!" she exclaimed.

Hannah wrinkled her nose at the partly eaten dead raccoon next to the porch, and she made a mental note to suggest to Mama that Walt should bury it behind the barn before it began to stink and offend the guests.

It was not merely that Walter was careless with Hunter that made Hannah sorry she had given her dog away. Walt had been feeding him only wildlife he had shot and using him as a working dog to keep the coons out of the corn or to follow the cows into the barn. These things, Hannah found, only made her indignant, though.

Hannah truly *missed* Hunter, for she loved him.
This was the crux of the matter. Oh, he was on his
chain at the end of the porch much of the day, true
enough. Many a time when Hannah went outside to
help a guest or to gather eggs or to milk Molly, she'd
stop to pet him lovingly. But no more could Hunter
run at her feet, his grand nose sniffing out a field
mouse or following a rabbit trail. No more did he
circle back after a romp in the field, then with excited glee wait trembling for Hannah to scratch his
ears.

No. Hunter was Walt's now.

But though Hannah had been trying to love Walt
by giving him Hunter, Hannah knew in the very
depths of her soul that something was dreadfully
wrong with this arrangement. Just what was
wrong, Hannah was not certain.

Walt had found Hunter very useful in the weeks
since Hannah had given her hound to him as a love
gift. A family of coons was making havoc of Papa's
cornfield, which he had planted for family food and
to feed Molly, Bullet, and the chickens. Papa and
Walt had tried shotguns and high-powered flash-
lights, but the coons seemed to sense the presence
of human hunters and stayed away. Papa and Walt
tried traps but learned when they found the traps
sprung and the bait stolen, that a coon is more
clever than a beaver. When one poor coon lost his
tail in a trap, Walt tied it to the scarecrow as a
warning to the others. "They're just laughing at it,
Walt," chuckled Mama, who could see humor even
in a desperate situation.

Next, Walt tried chaining Hunter between the
corn patch and the woods. That would scare the
raccoons off, surely. Hounds are mortal enemies to
coons.

That night the coons worked worse havoc than ever. Walt came in for breakfast leading a dejected hound on his chain, angrily scolding poor Hunter all the way.

"See here," said Papa, as the whole family followed him to the cornfield after breakfast. "Hunter did his best, but the coons got into the corn anyway." He pointed to trampled grass, where Hunter had made a perfect circle from his stake, at the end of his chain. "The coons soon figured out that Hunter was chained, and they stayed just out of reach and teased him." Papa picked up a half-eaten ear of corn just beyond Hunter's reach. "Looks like Hunter's only adding to their fun," he wryly observed.

"Why not just set Hunter loose in the corn, Papa?" Hannah asked.

"Fool dog would only run in the woods all night, chasin' rabbit trails," Walt interrupted.

"Walt's right, of course," Papa agreed. "But it's not fair to call a dog a fool for following his instincts," Papa added mildly correcting Walt.

So Papa himself decided that Hunter would work with him and Walt. They would take turns watching the cornfield, with Hunter on his chain to distract the coons. Papa and Walt each shot several, and the corn was saved at last.

"Here y' go, boy," cried Walt. Hannah watched one fall day as Walt tossed Hunter garbage left over from cleaning a rabbit. Walt had brought several rabbits home in recent weeks, but most of them he had buried in the garden after some days had passed and he had forgotten to ask Mama to fry them for his supper.

Hannah sighed sadly as Walt ran off to help

Papa without so much as stopping to pet Hunter or even to watch him enjoy his meal. As soon as Walt was out of sight, Hannah hopped down the porch steps. She hugged Hunter, fleas and all, then scratched him behind the ears where the beasties were biting worst.

"O-o-o-o-o," said Hunter, rolling his languid brown eyes up in love and appreciation.

"Casting all your care upon God, because he cares for you." That verse formed in Hannah's memory now, though she had not consciously tried to remember it. "Dear Lord, you take this care I've been carrying, worrying about Hunter, missing Hunter, wanting Walt to become more loving," Hannah prayed.

God answered at once. Hannah found herself peaceful and happy. What God would do to work things out, however, she had not a clue.

It was almost Walt's birthday—he would be fourteen. Nearly a man. Hannah smiled, realizing that her big brother had grown six inches and three shoe sizes in about a year.

She checked the old jewelry box that had been Grandma's. It was too small to hold anything but a few rings, so she used it for saving money. But now it didn't have enough to buy Walt a birthday present. Where did it all go? Then Hannah remembered, and a wave of anger swept over her. How could she be mad at Walt and love him at the same time? "I'll *never* understand myself!" Hannah cried aloud.

Hannah's mind went back two weeks, to the day she and Mama took the boat to Laketon to shop for groceries.

"Hunter needs a balanced diet," Hannah had

mildly protested to Walt when he had fed him a dead raccoon for breakfast. "Why don't you get him some dog food?"

"You're right," Walt had agreed. "Pick up a fifty-pound bag at the store for me will y'? I'll pay you when you get back—all my dough's upstairs in the attic," he said, with a nod toward Hannah's purse.

Walt had then hurried off to help Papa. But though Walt's Hunter had eaten some of the dog food, Walt hadn't remembered to pay Hannah.

"I'll just have to remind him," Hannah decided. She needed the money to buy her brother a present in Laketon tomorrow. "Fair enough," she told herself.

"I didn't want that ol' dog food, anyway," said Walt. "It was *your* idea. He gets along fine on table scraps an' stuff I shoot. What d' y' think dogs ate before people could buy dog food in supermarkets?"

Hannah's mind focused for a moment on a picture she'd once seen in *National Geographic*. It was of a mangy, skinny, underfed dog in a Third World country. With Walt tending Hunter, how long before he'd look like that? she wondered. But she said nothing.

"I'll make a deal with you," Walt went on. "You pay for the bag o' dog food, and you can have Hunter back. He doesn't like me, an' I ain't got time for him, anyway."

Hannah hugged a startled Walt, then kissed his cheek twice. "Thanks!" she cried. Rubbing her mouth, she remarked, "You're sprouting a beard, big brother!"

"Yep." Walt actually smiled. Then he strode off to help a guest with his luggage.

"Papa," Hannah said, after she found him in his

workshop repairing the snowmobile engine for winter use, "I'm terribly, terribly worried about Walter. An' I don't understand myself, either."

"Just when you've got a bull by the tail, he'll turn on you every time," Papa laughed, wiping the grease from his calloused fingers with an old rag.

"What do you mean?" Hannah was puzzled.

"Just when you think you understand a problem, it turns out it's bigger than you expect," Papa said, his merry eyes twinkling.

"I thought boys liked dogs." Hannah stated her problem.

"Exactly," said Papa. "But Walt isn't especially fond of Hunter. He *uses* him as a work dog, like he uses the John Deere. But he doesn't love him as a pet."

"That's right. But what would Walt like for a pet?" Hannah remembered that she still hadn't bought him a birthday gift, and she was determined to buy her brother *something*, even if it took her last penny.

"A girl." Papa winked at Hannah.

Hannah blushed. Her mind at once ran on the March morning when Walt seemed to enjoy very much the attention of their city cousins, Miquie and Minnie, as he harnessed Ebony. Only now did it dawn on Hannah that Walt had given the mice special attention because they were *girls* and not merely cousins.

"I'm not sure Walt's got that figured out, yet— that may partly explain his gruff attitude toward you," said Papa, smiling. "Boys usually love dogs, if they get them when the boy is only eight or ten. Older boys are so busy with the stuff of becoming a man that many of them will never learn to be affectionate with a dog."

"But *I* love Hunter dearly," Hannah protested, remembering that Papa had said that she was growing up, too.

"You're younger, and you have a different disposition," Papa said. "Besides, girls are more nurturing and affectionate than boys. God made 'em that way."

"Papa, you're a dear!" Hannah hugged him and kissed his cheek. She noticed that, like Walt, Papa had a stubble of whiskers. *I kinda think I like that*, Hannah decided.

Chapter Twenty

Who Walt Loves

"Papa's new boat is neat, huh?"

"Yeah." Walt all but ignored his sister as he skipped another flat rock onto Moosehead Lake.

Maybe he's just concentrating on improving his rock skipping, not having guys his age to play ball with, thought Hannah. After all, Moosehead is a big lake, and usually it's not calm enough to skip rocks except very early in the morning.

"That one skipped eight times," Hannah chirped, trying to encourage Walt in his solitary game.

"Yup."

"Had a chance to drive the new boat yet?"

"Nope."

Walt's one-word answers were beginning to bug Hannah, but she said nothing. Instead, she concentrated on admiring the twin-hull Chris-Craft fiberglass boat powered by two new Johnson Sea Horse motors. Papa had tied the boat up at the dock, taking pains to protect it with several new dock bumpers. Though the boat wasn't quite brand-new, Hannah knew that it would be a great boon to Papa's guide business. With it, Pap could take guests and their hunting, fishing, and camping gear beyond Beaver Island, far down Moosehead's vast expanse of water, to explore bays and lagoons for bass fishing or duck hunting.

It made perfect sense to Hannah, as she trudged toward the lodge, that Papa hadn't given either her or Walt permission to try out the fast, big boat. "I want to put the first scratch on that boat myself," she had heard Papa chuckle when he brought the boat home yesterday.

Hannah paused on the porch for a last look at Papa's fancy boat before going inside. She knew that later today Papa would go to Laketon to get a boatload of guests. Perhaps after the boat gets a few scuffs and dings from the tourists' luggage, Papa will let us try it out, she thought with a smile.

Walt wound up for a sidewinder fling of a flat rock as Hannah watched from the distance. He let it fly, and it skipped in a long arc towards the dock. "Tunk." The sound was barely audible, but Hannah could tell it hit hollow metal or fiberglass, not the solid wood posts of the dock. "Walt better be careful," she said half aloud, then scooted indoors.

※ ※ ※ ※ ※ ※ ※

Hannah paused from cleaning an upstairs bedroom at the sound of a motorboat starting up. It was Papa, and he was heading toward Laketon, evidently to meet his guests. But why is he using the *old* boat? she wondered.

Puzzled, Hannah stared at the new boat still tied to the dock. Odd, she thought—one motor's missing. The other looked out of place by itself.

She strained for a last look at Papa, now growing smaller in the distance. Then it dawned on her. The other outboard boat motor lay in the bottom of the old boat, its flashy red-and-silver paint glinting in the sun.

"Must've hit a floating log or something," Papa grumbled to Mama that evening. He had milked Molly, and he brought the pail of milk into the kitchen, where Mama and Hannah were preparing meals for his guests.

"How much is it going to cost?" Mama inquired.

"About a hundred dollars. The repairman's got to send to Skowhegan for parts, so it'll be out of commission for a couple of days. And it's not covered by the warranty, so I'll have to pay for the repair." Almost absent-mindedly Papa added, "Where's Walter?"

"Guess he's gone to his room," said Mama.

Papa headed for the stairs.

Uh-oh, thought Hannah.

But Papa's only reason for following Walt to his room, Hannah later learned, was to ask him why he'd left the barn early, forgetting to feed the calves.

Two days later, Papa came home with the repaired outboard motor. He clamped it onto the new boat beside the other new motor. Both motors ran perfectly as he circled out onto the lake, then puttered in toward the dock.

"This is really curious," Papa said at supper time. He fished a small piece of flat rock from his pocket and laid it on the kitchen table where the Parmenter family was eating after feeding their paying guests in the dining room.

"Just a piece of rock," Mama said, puzzled.

"The odd part is where it was found," Papa continued.

"Where was that?" Walt queried.

"The outboard motor repairman found it wedged between a couple of screws on the new motor in such a way that it damaged the carburetor. He said the only way it could have gotten there was if someone pounded it in there on purpose—or threw it at the motor."

"But who would want to sabotage your new boat?" Mama asked.

"Beats me," Papa shrugged.

"Oh," said Walter, looking troubled and his voice rising slightly as if he were remembering something. "Got t' check on the calves. I'm not sure I fed all of them."

Walt headed for the back door. He paused. "Papa, can you come to the barn with me?"

"Sure!" Papa left the room as if there were nothing unusual about Walt's request.

※ ※ ※ ※ ※ ※ ※

Walt seems happier than usual, Hannah thought to herself as she waited in the barn the next morning for Walter to finish milking Molly. Papa had left already with two men and their wives who wanted to see the fall foliage and take pictures of the reds and golds of the maples, birches, and poplars at the base of Mt. Kineo next to the lapping waves. Already the new boat was paying off, for one of Papa's guests was a well-paid professional photographer from New York who was doing a magazine layout and would pay Papa well for trips around Moosehead Lake.

"Since he got that new boat, Papa's been like a kid with a new toy," Hannah said. Her mind was on her brother, not the boat, but she thought Walt might talk with her if she talked about something that interested him.

"Sure is," Walt said enthusiastically. "He says he's taking our whole family for a ride Sunday afternoon. We can all take turns trying it out." He passed his sister the pail of milk, then reached for a pitchfork to feed the calves.

What's come over Walt? Hannah mused. She knew that 'taking turns' was not something that usually pleased Walt. Whether it was the tractor, the boat, the snowmobile, or riding Ebony, Walt wasn't happy unless he could tear off by himself, like a cowboy racing across the lonesome range. Now Walt seemed suddenly to have developed a new character trait: willingness to share without griping.

"Y' got a minute, sis?" Walt asked, interrupting Hannah's thoughts. His voice was soft, without a trace of the self-important sharpness that often made Hannah uneasy around her too-busy-to-be-friendly brother.

"Sure. Mama's got the kitchen under control, since the guests ate breakfast early to go with Papa. I'll help you with the calves." Hannah set the milk bucket on the grain bin and grabbed the grain scoop. "One scoop each—two for Molly, right?"

"Right," Walt agreed. "Did Papa tell you about the deal he got on that boat?"

"No, I guess not," Hannah said. What's Walt leading up to? she puzzled to herself.

"He bought it from Mrs. Ross, a widow from our church. Her husband bought the boat new and used it only a couple of times before he died. He had stored it, but burglars busted into his boathouse and ripped off both motors."

"That's why Papa had to buy new motors, I guess."

"Yep. Mrs. Ross sold him the boat real cheap, since the insurance company paid her for the stolen motors," Walt said.

After a brief pause, Walt spoke again. "You know something, Hannah? I've been kind o' like that boat."

"Oh. How's that?" Hannah caught her breath in excitement. This must be what Walt wanted to talk to her about.

"Lookin' good, like a new Chris-Craft," Walt said. "Carryin' my Bible to Sunday school, an' memorizing all those verses to win prizes."

Hannah nodded, recalling the summer before her family moved to Beaver Island when Walt won a free week at Camp Fair Haven.

"But like a boat without motors, I wasn't going anywhere!" Walt continued, almost angrily. "It took me breakin' that new Johnson Sea Horse Motor to bring me to my senses."

Hannah listened quietly.

"I was mad at Papa, and I had no right to be. He saved for *years* to buy that boat. He's been waitin' to drive a nice boat since you and I were just little kids. And all he'd asked us to do was wait another week."

"You didn't break it on purpose, did you Walt?" Hannah wanted to be sure she was hearing Walt right.

"Not on purpose. But I might's well have. I was mad at Papa, so I took a chance by throwin' rocks near his boat."

"And?"

"And Papa forgave me. He's not asking me to pay

for it—I'd just cleaned out my savings to buy some new fishing tackle."

Hannah nodded. She knew about the fishing tackle, but she hadn't asked to borrow it, since she knew how stingy Walt could be.

"It reminds me of how God forgave us, when Jesus paid for our sins on the cross when we couldn't pay," Walt added brightly. "Papa was quick to point out, though, that our sin debts are a lot higher than any money debt could be."

"That's for sure." Hannah smiled at her brother, who was looking at her like he wanted to say something more.

"Sis," he said at last. "Papa says the reason I give you such a hard time because I'm growing up and I don't understand myself."

"We're both growing up, Walt."

"I know," Walt chuckled. "Remember the time I hung you by your belt because you were throwing pine cones at me. I told you I figgered if you wanted to throw cones, you could just hang from the pine tree and *be a* cone."

"It was *your* belt, Walt," laughed Hannah. "Mama put it on me because I broke the elastic band in my pants."

"I must've lifted you ten feet with that block and tackle Papa had hung in the tree. You screamed your head off, scared silly."

"I was not! I was too mad to be scared!" Hannah bent to dump a scoop of grain into a calf's feed box, catching her jacket collar on a nail as she reached.

"Let me help you get loose." Walt pulled on Hannah's jacket. "Don't yank and twist; you'll rip your jacket," he warned, lifting the coat free.

Hannah straightened. Her shirt was full of calf

grain down her back clear to her waist, but she pretended not to notice, ignoring Walt's failed attempt to suppress a grin. Just then Hannah spied the garden hose that Walt had left uncoiled on the barn floor afer filling the animals' water buckets. She waited until Walt had picked up a bale of hay. Then she let him have it full in the face.

"I'll get you!" Walt yelled.

Too late. Hannah was already in the haymow, and she held the ladder out so Walt couldn't climb it.

"Awright, if I can't come up, you can't come down," he chortled, pulling the ladder from his sister's grasp and laying it on the barn floor.

Hannah watched Walt hurry into the tie-up, where the animals' body heat would keep him warm while he wrung the water out of his flannel shirt. She scurried across the hay bales to the barn's rear wall, where a small window opened onto the low roof of Papa's workshop. Hannah slid the window open and crawled outdoors onto the roof. Reaching back inside, she pulled a hay bale across the opening, then let the sash drop. Walt can bring the milk to the house, she decided, for by now the calf grain had migrated throughout all her clothing.

※ ※ ※ ※ ※ ※ ※

"What on earth happened to you, big brother?" Hannah had changed her clothes, then gone back downstairs and gotten out the clean milk bottles, all before Walt entered the kitchen lugging the pail of milk.

"You rascal! You're no girl, you're a squirrel!"

"Shh. I've managed to fool Mama for 'most 12 years. She thinks I'm human."

"I thought you'd hid in the hay, so I climbed into the haymow," Walt said, gesturing at his shirt, still damp and now covered with chaff. "I was afraid that you'd get hurt trying to get down without a ladder."

"Walt, you're a dear, even if you are my brother. I didn't know you cared," Hannah added, giving him a quick hug.

"Well, this'll sound crazy. But I think you're pretty nice sis." Walt gave her a peck on the cheek. "Love y', Han," he said, turning to fill the bottles from the pail.

Hannah chuckled to herself, watching Walt splash milk on the kitchen counter as he poured milk from a ten-quart pail into old-fashioned, narrow-necked bottles without using a funnel, as he had often seen Papa do. Papa, she knew, could fill a row of bottles without spilling a drop.